ALSO BY KENJI JASPER

Dark

DAKOTA GRAND

a novel

KENJI JASPER

Harlem Moon
Broadway Books
New York

Designed by Chris Welch

ISBN 0-7394-2999-x

PRINTED IN THE UNITED STATES OF AMERICA

FOR WOOD, MURPH, AND MIKE

WE SAW THE YEAR THAT REALLY CHANGED EVERYTHING

First and always, I thank the Creator, for getting me through this life, and more drafts of this book than I want to count. Thanks to my insatiable editor, Gerry Howard, for pushing me until he *got* this book. I adore my earth-shaking agent Gloria Loomis and her wonderful assistant, Katherine Fausset. Thanks to all my readers: Gregory L. Johnson, Jr., Nadja and Jessica, DarkBlue36, B-Man, Tahra Chatard, Roberto Johnson, Rebecca Levine, Ms. Jackson (over in the UK), and the delicious flutterings of the one and only Ms. Butterfly Webb. Additional shout-outs go to Knox, Tamesha, Konata, Mill, Gaff, Coco and Joshua, Natalie and Gabrielle, Big Bob Meadows, Kaypri, Abby, Adele, J. Sanders, Cara Grayer, Rebeccah Bennett (since I can never find you), Anika Cazenave, and most important, to the people of Washington, D.C., for reminding me of how much love you give to your own.

START

NEW YORK CITY is a universe all to itself, an independent entity jam-packed with a wide assortment of stars and planets. Its galaxies are called boroughs. Suspension bridges serve as intergalactic conduits that take you from one quadrant to the next.

But it's not the place to be if you really want to *live*. There are no porches to sit on while you watch your neighbors moving to and fro. All the summertime lemonade and iced tea comes from powder. No one says thank you, replacing the words with a blank stare or a hanging jaw with no sound coming out of it. Good cornbread, grits, and greens are too hard to find. And your time is always running out.

I lived on Planet Hip-Hop, that tiny spinning ball that everybody talks about. It's the one that the white kids in Kentucky model their lives after, the one that pays for many emperors' new robes, while gradually eroding itself in the process.

My job on the planet was to write. I was supposed to analyze the music that hip-hop made and come up with answers, interviews, opinions, inside stories. And for a while I was up to the task, because I was good, really good.

I came through the ranks like a force of nature, rising from a foot soldier to a captain in the time it took most to get their first piece published. I became the job, abandoning all senses of love, of family, and of self, to be a part of the new greatest show on earth. My stories usually made the covers, or at least the featured articles page. People knew me. Girls liked me. But at some point that stopped being enough to keep me going.

The whole scene started to feel empty. We bobbed our heads to the music out of habit instead of enjoyment. Artists kicked out product like machines. It was no longer created, only developed, assembled, and shipped. We writers were just the folks who did the press kits.

The little money we got couldn't fill the widening gaps. Our sense of life, of the world, became muted, like touching fine furniture when it's under a plastic cover. Then my day of reckoning came. And I needed things to be different. But I went too far to try and change them. I did find love, again. But I learned that one person alone can't change a game. He can only change himself.

WINTER

REMEMBER THE day when it started. It was just a few weeks before winter and I was sitting in a familiar place, the vinyl-cushion-covered bench in the Raw Records waiting area. Hours had passed and my back had started to ache from sitting too long. The olive-skinned, auburn-hair-weaved receptionist looked right through me as she sucked up company time yapping to a friend, complaining that some specific "he" was never going to treat her right. There were several gold and platinum plaques on the walls around me. I looked at my watch and it said three-thirty. I had been there since one-fifteen.

"They're just running a little late," the girl interjected. Her tight-fitting pants were the color of fresh mangoes and her angora sweater clung to her skinny, shapeless upper frame. "They should be here soon."

She had said that four times since I'd arrived, and Diversion, as the group was called, had yet to show themselves. The piece was a favor for a friend at *Fluff* magazine. And I needed the money. So I was going to wait until they either showed up or told me that I'd have to reschedule.

The entrance doors finally flung open when I was on the verge of turning to stone. The manager came first and the four teenage boys dragged behind him like little kids on their way to the dentist for cavities.

"Yo, so sorry man!" the manager explained. "We had this in-store at the Virgin Records downtown and the honeys just wouldn't let them loose." Two of the boys developed grins, knowing that they were now stars.

"It's all right," I said politely. "Y'all ready to do this?"

"Then let's go," one of them said. I think that his name was Kerry.

If I had read the press packet I would have known more about them, where they were from and how they'd ended up being feature material for a magazine like *Fluff*. But I hadn't read a thing. I'd told myself that I didn't need it, that they were just another carbon-copy cutout R&B group. I could easily fill in the blanks in front of the laptop back at my apartment.

We worked our way through the mazes of offices into

a small conference room, where we all took seats in plush leather chairs. The manager, a man with a Brooklyn accent who looked old enough to be my father, shut the door after we entered. I wanted to get it over with, write the piece, pick up my check in about a month, and forget all about this Diversion. So I pulled my first question.

"So tell me about how—"

The door opened before I could finish and the same little publicity girl with the mango pants was standing there.

"I'm sorry but I'm going to need Kerry, Sam, and Bruce. *Seventeen* just got here." My article had been superseded by the mainstream, by little white girls with fantasies about black boys who could sing, dance, and gyrate their midsections. There was obviously no loyalty from Raw, even though *Fluff* had been giving their artists maximum exposure from the beginning.

"Well *Seventeen* needs to wait," I replied, more than pissed off. "I've been waiting to do this for—"

"We're going to bring them back," she said politely, to shut me up. "They'll be back in a few minutes."

The designated boys rose from their seats like soldiers ready to go into battle. They filed behind the mango girl and shut the heavy wood door behind them. I'd been left with Kamau, the one kid who never sang lead, and the manager. I asked them all the questions I could think of, a half hour's worth, waiting for the other three to return. But they didn't.

I should've gone to find the head publicist, to complain, to reschedule, to find the *Seventeen* people and beat their heads in with my recorder. But instead I shook the two subjects' hands and left the conference room. I found my way to the front door, and went through it. I was tired of the same ole game. The usual me could've stayed there for five more hours without blinking.

On the street I made a payphone call to Layla, the editor I was helping, and told her that my recorder had malfunctioned, that I was going to have to do the interview over. She expressed her disappointment but said she understood. I dropped the Diversion interview tape into the garbage basket next to the payphone. Then a smile found its way to my face.

I stood on 44th and Broadway, right in the middle of the new Times Square, the neon-lighted, multimedia billboard evil Emperor Giuliani had built for us, and took in a breath of polluted air. I wasn't sure of what to do for the rest of the day. But Diversion quickly faded from my mind like a forgettable scene in cinema.

Right there I decided that I couldn't do it anymore, that I'd had enough. A $500 pain-in-the-ass payday wasn't enough to buy my soul. Things had to change, get better. It didn't have to happen right then. But it had to happen. I was afraid of what I'd do if it didn't.

"So how'd you get started," a voice asked me weeks later, at a cheap but trendy Indian restaurant on the East Side called the Bindhi Bistro.

I'd started out in the game just like everyone else. I'd gotten tired of being the piranha writer in Atlanta's little goldfish pond. So I stacked some loot, packed all that I could carry, and left the rest at the curb in front of my newly vacant efficiency on Cascade Road. Then I raced to catch a student discount flight to La Guardia Airport in Queens, where no one was waiting to greet me.

I carried two heavy gym bags and a backpack on a crowded M30 bus to Manhattan and saw how the project buildings along the East River seemed almost as tall as the 'scrapers in midtown. The voices around me were loud and abrasive. The black and brown babies in strollers and carriers flailed their arms and legs in struggle, as if they wanted to escape. Everything seemed to be covered in soot.

But the immediate present didn't matter. I had it all figured out. I gave myself the pen name Dakota Grand and had a portfolio full of clips that vouched for that writer's existence. When you gave yourself a pen name it was like you got to be someone entirely different. It was so easy to understand why rappers did the same thing.

I also had a list of numbers and addresses from the old to connect with the new. And there was a floor to sleep on in a cramped space at 127th and Lenox. But it wasn't until later that I realized the gravity of what I did. In making that hajj to the Apple, I had been forever transfigured. I instantly turned into a platinum icon to be smiled upon by everyone back home. Well, almost everyone.

Ma didn't approve. But I decided that she was just one against the many who did. But she still sent checks when I needed them. And Pop didn't have any way of noticing my change of residence. He didn't even have a window in his cell.

The first year slurred by like drunken speech. I wore retail name tags during the day and did interviews on my lunch breaks for magazines you've never heard of. It was like getting the Pulitzer when I got my first hundred words in a book people actually read. Instead of eating $3 Chinese takeout from that same place on 132nd, I started to have enough for the $4 Dominican and falafel meals closer to home.

Then I moved to my own cramped space, where stray cats fought and made noises in the garbage-filled courtyard beneath my apartment at night. And eventually it got easier. I got more free records, more invitations to release parties, more guests allowed to accompany me at premier events. Before I knew it three years had passed. I had moved to Brooklyn. And someone wanted to know how I had done it.

"You gotta forget everything you learned down

there," I said to the neophyte. As I spoke I couldn't remember his name. I didn't want to ask him a third time. "You gotta forget all that and learn what you need to survive up here. Up here you either got the talent or you don't. The sooner you figure out which it is the better."

How was I supposed to give someone advice about something I still just barely knew myself? How could I explain to the freshman before me that the life he wanted to live, the life *I* was living, was nothing but smoke and mirrors, the frames they cut out of music videos for not being flashy enough? Mic-holders held the spotlight. Nobody cared about the men with pens.

Massai Morris, the bright-eyed rookie before me, had almost been a friend once. So I owed him more than two sentences when I bumped into him at the *Maintain* magazine website launch party. He had been the only one in the room not infected by the idle chatter disease, or the nasty Heineken breath that came with it. I gave him one of my business cards, the ones with the raised lettering on the glossy cream surface, and told him that we should have lunch.

A month had passed since then. And as I looked at him there, his peach fuzz stuck to his chin like lint, I noticed that the shape-up across the front of his caesar was lopsided. His red-and-black plaid shirt had been worn far too many times. I felt bad for what he was about to go through.

I knew all the unreturned calls he would make, all the nights he'd spend arguing with brainless bouncers and self-righteous security guards over whether or not he was on the press list. I couldn't just come out and tell him that he was never going to get his checks on time, or that his credit rating would fall beneath absolute zero in his first six months. I couldn't tell him any of that, because it was too soon for him to really understand.

But Morris was lucky. When I'd made my hajj to the unholy land, the only advice I'd gotten about New York had come from Antoine, my barber at the shop on Brawley Drive, right down the street from where I'd dropped out of college. Antoine had lived in New York for two weeks while he was house-sitting for an out-of-town aunt in Queens. He told me that New York was the kind of place where you had to "show no fear and take no prisoners."

I took that to mean that it thrived on your weaknesses and waited for you to make mistakes. From what he said I imagined that the Apple could bend and twist, your better-than-average life until it folded and curled into your own personal hell. After those words of encouragement Antoine finished blocking the hair on the back of my neck and I was on my way to the airport.

"You came up here and did your thing," Morris said with his accent twanging just as hard as my own. I still hadn't let the "Beast of the East" take the south out of me. He passed me his *Maintain* magazine research associate business card. He glowed at having something to hand to people, even if it screamed that he was doing the two-step in a salsa competition.

"You look different," he added while studying my face between sips, "like you been through some shit up here." I looked around the restaurant to search for an appropriate answer. But there was nothing for me in the white tablecloths or the plastic flower arrangements in the front window. Morris gave a quick nod to someone he knew on the other side of the room. I could remember when the place had served Italian instead of Indian two years before.

If he wanted to know the truth it had been the weed and the cigarettes and the Hennessy. It was the confused and confusing girls who picked and shoveled their way toward their dreams. It was the late nights and hangover mornings. If I looked different it was because I had been stripped down to nothing but the essentials.

There were no more idealistic dorm room discussions about pure art and Richard Wright and why Ralph Ellison spent the rest of his life trying to write a second book. In the Apple I just wanted respect, the regular exchange of fluids with a girl of choice, and enough money to keep my checks from bouncing. But I found an answer that would suit him.

"It's hectic up here," I said coldly. "That's all I can say about it. It's hectic."

His expression changed as I let out a sigh. He'd gotten the point. He looked at his watch and saw that he also had to get back to his office. I had to get to my interview.

"Well, if you need anything from me you know you can holler at me," he said as he rose from the table, plopping down just enough for both lunches and a skimpy tip. I shook his hand like a businessman. Beyond the exit door we walked in opposite directions.

It wasn't until after he was out of range that I remembered how good of a writer he'd been at the college paper. I really did wish him the best. In the face of "the Life," he was going to need it.

The winter hawk clawed at me as I slid down Third Avenue like a skate on ice, my leather jacket zipped to the neck and my Braves hat pulled down and slightly to the left, the way I always wore it. I played the cab game for nearly twenty minutes before a graying white man my father's age braked at the corner of Third Avenue and 32nd. Before I got into the cab I looked around at the East Side, at the sandstone and brick buildings that surrounded the Empire State a few streets over. The clock on the Citibank a block up read 2:15. I had to hurry. We headed towards Brooklyn at warp 6.

It wasn't until we cleared a bottleneck at Atlantic and

Flatbush Avenue that I realized that I hadn't written down a single question. I had gotten to the point where I usually just made up questions on the spot for my interviews. The answers were usually all the same anyway. But this one was too important for that.

Mirage had been the man I called my hero. And my hero, along with his often detached and rumored-to-be-starstruck partner 9–9, had just closed the book on one of the most successful underground hip-hop groups of the decade, Arbor Day. Some people still hadn't figured out that they'd named themselves that because of all the cannabis trees they smoked.

But the breakup story had gotten deeper when Mirage also divorced his wife, an R&B singer whose name no one ever seemed to remember. Both events had happened six weeks before he was to release his first solo album. Someone had to pick up the pieces and *The Magazine* had designated me as the one to do it.

Mirage, my hero, was supposed to be the nice guy of the duo. He was the one who cracked the occasional smile in photographs, the one who was seen signing every autograph and who had reportedly donated more money to charities than most people, much less rappers. But it was 9–9's Teflon persona and misogynistic lyrics that pulled millions of fans through the group's four gold albums. I'd bought each of the four the day it came out. I also had two full tapes' worth of unreleased tracks I'd picked up from various sources over the years. Arbor Day was the Holy Grail I'd come to the city in hopes of covering, the one-armed man in my *Fugitive* life. So I was finally on my way to the next level.

Getting to write for *The Magazine* wasn't easy. If you didn't have a name editors weren't too excited about throwing you work. But as soon as I heard about the breakup from one of my sources I typed up a quick proposal, trained into the city, and walked it right into their offices, where I waited for almost two hours before Chad, the music editor, came out.

"You definitely have patience and persistence," Chad said while skimming through the almost twenty articles in my portfolio. A thirty-something white boy with horn-rimmed glasses and a Green day T-shirt, he looked like he was trying to be nineteen for the rest of his life, with very little success.

"Thanks," I replied nervously.

"You know I'd thought about doin' a piece on them once," he said nostalgically. "Right after the *High Times* album came out. But the new Tribe album hit that same month and the whole thing got lost in the shuffle."

"People just didn't feel that record the way they should have," I said. "I think they're the only people who got away with sampling Sinatra."

"You're probably right," he grinned. "So you're looking for your shot at the big time, huh?"

The question made me feel like I was a nobody, like all the work I'd done had meant nothing to him. He'd seen the covers and the profiles I'd done, the conference panels I'd taken part in. And to him I was still just a little fish.

"I been tryin' for a long time," I replied earnestly. He glanced down at my portfolio before he zipped it up and handed it back to me. I was choking on the suspense.

"You right. *High Times* is the best shit they ever did. *The Source* was wrong for trashing it," he scowled, as if the two year-old review was still fresh in his mind. "Give me twenty-five hundred words. I'll set up the interview and give you a call tomorrow."

He called me the next day with a time, address, and contact person for the meeting. I told him that I could get everything else. I had quotes and background sources I'd been saving for years, early news clippings and videotape. I told Chad that no one could do it the way I could. And he believed me.

I smiled as I shook his hand, looking more like an overeager Jimmy Olson than a decorated vet in the game. My three years would have been ten in any other business.

But getting the article hadn't happened the way I'd imagined it. I'd wanted to track Mirage down on my own, catch him record shopping or in the grocery store. I wished that I could have stopped him on the spot and told him that I could write a piece unlike anything, something that would tell his fans who he really was. I wished that I could have seen him say yes and write down his home number, so that we could talk about his career over Heinekens at his favorite bar. Then the editors would have come to me, begging to publish the piece under their various banners.

But things didn't work that way in the music journalism of 1999, at least not after rappers started selling millions of records, turning up in movies, and endorsing brands and products. The game now included managers and publicists, label executives and hangers-on galore. Each and every one of them was employed to keep you, the writer, the critic, the fan, from your intended target. And more often than not they succeeded.

But all someone like Chad had to do was make a phone call and it was done. Chad had one of the biggest music magazines in the country behind him. It would've taken months to set it up anywhere else.

The interview was going to be just the two of us. I told his publicist that it would be "just a few questions and answers in the studio" and that we wanted to see him at work on his first solo album. Publicists got paid to lie so writers never told them the truth. And Mandy, who sounded like the type to grab her purse in an elevator with any nonclient black person, was quick to oblige me once I had *The Magazine*'s blessing.

The cab rocketed down Flatbush through a string of green lights. The afternoon traffic was light as we looped around Grand Army Plaza and then past the Ebbets Field projects. By the time we turned onto Ocean Avenue I had scribbled down thirteen questions on my notepad, hoping that their answers would be more than enough to fill the ninety minutes of tape I had in my recorder. Chad had called early that morning to say that the piece has been marked as a possible cover in their afternoon editorial meeting. But it had to be done right. I missed the name of the cross street where the yellow car applied its brakes.

I left the driver with $25 for a $20 ride, pretending like I could afford it, and got out of the sputtering vehicle just before it took off. Manhattan cabbies hated driving into Brooklyn. I stood there and watched the yellow car fade into the distance.

Something stopped me from going in right away, even as the bitter cold dug its way into my clean-shaven cheeks. I took a moment to stare at the building where my career was about to change. From the outside the studio looked small, definitely too small for someone like Mirage, who had been recording for almost a decade. But I was sure there was a reason for him being there. And that was one of the many things I intended to find out before I left. A deep blue 4.6 Range Rover and an '89 Honda Accord sat parallel to each other in the otherwise empty parking lot. I assumed that the Rover was Mirage's.

I approached the plate-glass door with an even blend of confidence and caution. But I relaxed at the sight of the smiling short-skirted receptionist, particularly as she got up from her seat and walked over to open the door for me. I pushed record just as I entered.

My mentor Scott had always told me that if you had your tape running early you had a chance of getting a free piece of gossip, an album release date, samples of a work-in-progress, or any of the other little goodies editors would die for. It was something I'd kept in mind ever since I took his workshop at City College, and more important since he'd seemingly dedicated much of his little free time to trying to make me a better writer, an Obi-Wan for the kid from Atlanta who he thought might have been the last Jedi.

"You must be Mr. Grand," she said, grinning. "He's in the back." She pointed to the wide passageway to her left. I turned and began my slow drag down the corridor, passing through the tunnel of awards and plaques that led to Studio C.

A mumbling hum came from the room in question. It was the kind of hum a mother made while moving from one task to the next. But this time it came from Mirage's closed lips. He was sitting in the middle of the room, perfectly centered between the engineer's booth and the microphone. A small folding table had been erected before him to hold a huge bag of weed. And next to the bag were a boxcutter, a split-open cigar, a blue ceramic ashtray, and a bottle of Poland Spring water, all ordered in a perfect row like a surgeon's tools.

He had yet to see me when he placed a sampling of the dark green mass onto the cigar wrapper, broke it up, and scraped it into an even line to begin the rolling process. Minutes later he ran a lighter under the wet edges and lit the spliff. To my left the engineer's booth was dark and the stereo against the soundproofed wall was on mute. The colored lights on the equalizer jumped up and down in silence. He exhaled a cloud of smoke and finally noticed me standing there.

Visine couldn't have helped his eyes and his lips were nearly purple from his smoking, much darker than they seemed in his videos. His clothes, a blue plaid Phat Farm button-up and matching jeans, looked like they'd been slept in, and the dreads that had covered his dome for Arbor Day's supposedly final album, *Timber!*, had been replaced by a short peasy afro. The unkempt hair perfectly matched his severely stubbled face. He grinned.

Arbor Day always came off like they were smarter than everyone else. They'd sampled Sinatra's "My Way" and played it backwards and then sped it up for a song called "Razor Blade" about a fatal battle shootout on a street corner. They interwove flutes and marimbas with dark drums and bass lines. They brought in classically trained sopranos to sing over flamenco guitar loops and African djembes. Arbor Day made music that you sat and *listened* to.

And then there were their videos. They didn't wear thick gold ropes or shoot their videos in the projects to represent. The clip for their first single ever, "On a Roll," was shot on a golf course where they had the president of their record label walking around behind them as their caddy. While everyone else was trying to look tough in front of graffiti murals, Mirage and 9–9 were seen observing a wedding from the back of the chapel and rhyming from the top of a Mount Rushmore with their faces carved into the stone. Like me, they took it beyond the limits. But unlike me, they'd already made it.

"So you ready?" he asked as if I was the one who had to answer the questions. I nodded. The reels on my recorder were in motion.

"I'll start off with what everyone is going to ask you—"

"I don't know why we broke up," he said before I could finish. The spliff burned out and he relit it. "I been in here almost every day for three weeks trying to figure it out. I been tryin' to write the rhyme that'll explain it to the fans but every time I try I always seem to leave somethin' out."

He was in no way a small man, at least 6'2", 250 lbs.

It had always been strange to me how calm he had always seemed in the public view. In a relatively long career he'd never seen a single scandal, arrest, or lawsuit.

"It was like one day me and 9 are in the studio workin' on a song and the next thing I know I'm at a new label signin' a solo deal. You know I said I'd never do a solo record? I mean—I guess I saw it happening. We was getting on each other's nerves half the time, like some old-ass couple that don't know how to stop arguing. So we just ended it. As for my wife, who I know you gonna ask about, it was like the same thing except she was the one who woke up and said that she wasn't cool with it anymore. She was like, 'Michael, you promised me that shit would settle down.' I had promised and I didn't live up to it. Her career wasn't really going so well. I mean her group broke up. She was in a bad contract. I just think she wanted to make a new start, break away from everything, and I wasn't there to give her the support she needed. Now I wake up in a big house all by myself."

Most artists I'd interviewed always gave the same answers. Even if it wasn't intentional they anticipated what was important, what the writer wanted to know, or exploit. So they fed you what they thought you wanted to hear like it was a plate of prime rib and Cristal. But as I listened I had a feeling that I was hearing something that no one else had. And as Arbor Day fan #1, that meant more than he would ever know.

"What did your marriage teach you about love?" I wasn't sure where the question had come from. But it was a good one to ask.

He paused for a few moments, looking as if he'd misplaced the answer and was trying to find it again. He finally sighed and gave up the search.

"I mean, you see your girl walk down that aisle with that dress and veil and you see your boys standin' beside you with tuxedos and shoes and you know that you love this woman more than any of the other hoes, more than anything."

He paused and rolled up the sleeve of his sweater to point to the full-color tattoo of his ex-wife's face printed onto his thick left biceps.

"But in the end marriage ain't really got shit to do with love. It's about trust. Can you trust this woman to be with you for the rest of your life? Can you trust her to raise your seeds? I mean you buy that ring when you think you know. You say those vows when you're sure. But you don't know until you put it into practice. So it's like one day the two of you livin' like Cliff and Claire Huxtable and the next thing you know your man is callin' you up sayin' he seen your wife goin' into a hotel wit' somebody else."

His voice dragged like a record playing slightly below speed. His spliff burned quickly as he took in and released smoke like it was pure oxygen. Not once did he offer me a hit. So I lit up a Newport and dealt with it.

"Is that how it happened with you?"

"Nah," he said, seeming as if he was proud of himself for painting such a picture. "It was more like we just . . . faded away. She knew my life. She knew what I did and she said that she understood. But when I started producin' more and doin' more shows it started getting hard for her to deal, even though we were in the same business. We fought over stupid shit. Not even about money. It had been her idea to sign the pre-nup. You know she took me to my favorite restaurant to tell me she was leaving. Said I'd be calm about it that way like I was Jerry Maguire or some shit. I mean I didn't even see it comin'. All the ass that was out there on the road and she was all I thought about, my only focus."

I checked to make sure the tape was still running, which it was. He wasn't talking to me anymore, but someone closer to him who should have been sitting in my chair. He should have said those things to his best friend, his father, a psychiatrist. But I was a journalist writing the cover story of my young career. I had to tell the truth and print what the *The Magazine*'s readers wanted to know. I had done it in the 234 articles before this one and it couldn't stop just because my favorite rap star was sitting in front of me. Time passed and more words were recorded. In some ways it felt unreal, like something I'd dreamed up on the way to one of my dead-end day jobs.

"No matter how hard I tried, all of it went into the music," he continued. "When I first started working on this album I wanted to make something beautiful." He stubbed the roach into the cluttered ashtray in front of him. "I wanted to do something that people wasn't expectin', somethin' different from what me and 9 had done on all those albums. The first few songs were dope and I was happy. But one day I was sittin' in here thinkin' about my life. When you get in this business you see too many foul things and no matter how hard you try to forget, those things you see affect you in a lot of different ways."

"Like what, for example?"

He paused as recollection tightened its grip on his memory.

"I mean, I've seen managers get their artists on tape with other men and other girls, makin' them sign bad contracts to keep them from sendin' the tapes to the media. I seen record execs make interns strip for them at private parties, run trains on them, and ask them to get coffee for them at work on Monday. I've seen fans bring dope to shows and give it to their junkie idols backstage. And I'm not just talkin' about weed either. When you sign a contract and sell some records they try to make you into an idol god. Then you struggle with all the other idols so you can be worshiped the most.

"I didn't want to be nobody's idol from the beginning. I just wanted to make records that people liked. So did 9. But after a while 9 started gettin' caught up in everything else but getting the music done. We started workin' together less and less. By the last album he would just come in, do his verses, and leave until it was time to go on tour. He was busy fuckin' wit' models and tryin' to get in movies."

He paused again, his eyes staring at the demons just over my shoulder. It was almost scary, the way I understood him. Those same interns he talked about were the ones who walked me to conference rooms for interviews, who checked me off on press lists and took messages for publicists. I knew all the stories about artists being extorted, about people ending up broke working at supermarkets because they never had the sense to learn the business. But most of all I understood that spinning feeling, that merry-go-round of the same people and places that eventually brought you nothing but dizziness. It was my life too. And I wanted out of it in the same way that he did.

"So I had all of that on my mind," he continued. "I couldn't just make something beautiful. I had to tell the truth. I told my ex-wife the truth. I told 9 the truth. Now everybody else needs to hear what I have to say. So you wanna hear what I got done?"

I nodded as he stood up and walked over to the stereo in the corner. He turned on the power and pushed play. By the time the tape finished I thought I was high. I had never heard anything like it. It was beyond gold and platinum. It was beyond styles and trends. It was classic, in the purest form of the word, the greatest listening privilege I had ever been afforded. And I had heard it first. All the evidence had been safely recorded on tape. I was now on my way and nothing was going to stop me.

We shook hands at the door to Studio C and I was back on the streets, asking passersby how I could get to the No. 2 train. I wished I hadn't spent the extra five on the cab as hunger burned deep in my stomach.

■ ■ ■

THERE WAS SOMETHING comforting about the frigid air as it kissed my face on the other side of the plate-glass entrance. At the curb I lit a cigarette and thought about the hour that had just gone by. I had traveled to another realm where Mirage's words were the air that filled my lungs. It was there on that corner that my story was conceived. But it wouldn't be born until a few days later, in the confines of my too expensive one-bedroom in Clinton Hill, Brooklyn.

I started my multiblock hike up to the avenue where I was told I could find a train. I liked walking. It always gave me time to watch other people's lives as they passed by me. On trains I flew past everything, including things I didn't want to miss.

The years had passed like hours. It hadn't been that way at home. There, every day went by with a memory to go with it: Grandma's macaroni and cheese on Sunday, backed-up traffic on Ashby Street outside of 112 and Club 559 on the weekends. When I wrote something down there back then, people remembered and talked about it weeks after it was published.

But there were ghosts at home too, memories of people, places and decisions that I wanted to put behind me. In New York, you could be who you wanted to be. There was no one down the street or around the corner to rub your nose in the past, to remind you of the person you once were.

It seemed warmer on the other side of the station turnstiles, even though I could still see my breath. I looked up at the gray strips of dried paint hanging from the neglected ceiling above the train platform. The Manhattan-bound side was relatively empty. I took a seat on the first of two sectioned wood benches and waited. Someone was whistling somewhere, the sound echoing into the tunnels that carried us to and fro beneath the city.

"Yowhereyoufromshortie?" the man demanded to the object of his affection, a tiny Jamaican girl with a diamond in her left nostril and a collection of gold jewelry that rivaled Mr. T's. There wasn't a single pause between his words.

"I'm from here," she replied. "I just been in Alabama for a few years livin' with my fatha."

I got up and began to walk down towards the other end of the platform, closer to where the back of the train would stop when it arrived. I had heard their conversation before. It had come from so many different mouths at different times and places. Every once in a while it even came from my own lips.

There were only two outcomes. She would either blow him off or give him the number. If he got between her thighs he'd either slither away or they'd fall in love, become a husband and wife with kids. More than likely she'd dismiss him like a class and their individual lives would keep running in place like hamsters on a treadmill. Eight million stories and most of them were repeats.

I couldn't judge them because I was just as guilty as the next man. After all, I did work in the media and there were plenty of girls who went for that kind of thing. It was always a feather in your cap to be able to get front-row seats and backstage passes with just a few phone calls. But I only hit a home run once or twice a season.

But my less-than-player status more than likely stemmed from the fact that I never played that "connected guy" card when I first met someone. And connected guys were what most girls went for. And if you weren't connected then you had to be a thug. Anyone in the middle of those two extremes had to work twice as hard to keep their lives from being lonely.

Usually I didn't even tell girls what I did. I liked being Clark Kent. I approached them with "honesty," told them what I knew they wanted to hear, and then kept them moving in and out of my front door like it was a revolving entrance. That was me at my best. At my worst I was calling my friend Maya on late Thursday nights hoping that she'd have a female friend in town who wanted to go out, someone full of empty words who didn't care who I was beneath the costume I'd created.

The duo's voice droned off and the platform seemed to stretch forever as I walked its length. The ancient concrete beneath me had supported millions of Brooklynites without once being thanked. I'd heard that the subway was more than a hundred years old and wondered how many ghosts and spirits might lurk within its tunnels.

But then I heard it. It came like a song from the heavens or a shot fired in the midst of confusion. It was the sound of a woman, a woman hocking a piece of gum onto the tracks in front of her. It was so loud that I had to turn and look.

There wasn't a shade of brown dark enough to describe her complexion. Nor was there an adjective that captured the embarrassed grin she flashed when she saw that there was a witness to her uncouth action. She looked like she might have been from my neck of the woods, a blackberry-colored Southern belle stuck in the northern jungle while trying to make all her special dreams real. But I was wrong.

"It's all right," I said. "I ain't gonna tell nobody."

"Thank you," she said after a pause. "Wouldn't want anybody thinking I was unladylike."

Her lips were full but not thick, her eyes narrow but not Asian. And she had a Spanish accent. So I took the opportunity to switch over to her tongue. My Spanish minor in college had come in handy many a night at the Latin clubs, when they actually understood what I was saying. I asked her where she was from.

"*Soy de Cuba*," she replied, affirming my suspicions. Puerto Ricans and Dominicans didn't look like her. To think of it, no woman I'd ever seen had looked like her.

"So what you doin' down here?" I asked.

"Seein' my friend."

"Can I be your friend too then?"

"You don't seem like the type to take friendship seriously."

"What makes you say that?"

"Am I wrong?"

I wanted to lie but something in her face said that the truth couldn't hurt her.

"No."

Her chocolate nose was perfectly medium.

"So then what do you really want me for?"

I was caught off guard. Before I could answer, our train rushed into the station. She walked ahead of me, which gave me a chance to take a closer look. Her wool slacks hugged her obviously well-toned thighs and her ass was wide and round. The bubble coat covering her upper frame concealed the rest of the package. The train slowed to a stop and the doors slid open. We entered and I sat right next to her. I had to try.

"I guess you weren't expecting a real conversation," she said in response to my silence.

"I was just coming up with a good answer, that's all, like us goin' out to dinner or the movies, or whatever you want."

"But why?" she asked again, drilling beneath the pretense most girls naturally thought was the truth.

"Because you're impressin' me. 'Cause you can spit gum on train tracks and still be sexy."

Her grin opened into a smile.

"You're funny," she said.

"So where you goin'?" I asked.

"Back to work," she said. "I took a long lunch."

"Lunch in Brooklyn?" I asked.

"Yes. I work at Borough Hall, only a few stops from home."

"Well, if I knew you were gonna be out here I woulda took you to lunch myself."

"I gotta give you credit," she said as she shook her head. "You're *really* trying your best."

"A woman like you doesn't deserve any less."

"And how do you know what kind of woman I am? You haven't even known me for five minutes."

I looked at my watch.

"You're right. It's four and a half and counting."

She grinned again. I grinned back. I was on my way to the winner's circle.

"So where do you live?"

"Crown Heights."

"I'm not over there a lot. But I got some friends who are."

"I like it. I've lived there with my uncle since I came here."

"How long you been here?"

"Five years."

"I been here for two years and I still don't know if I like it."

"That probably means you don't."

"Why do you say that?"

"Most people know if they like something or not from the very beginning. They just don't want to admit it to themselves."

"I guess that's true. So what do you do, Ms. . . ." That was the point where she was supposed to tell me her name.

"You know, I've never met a guy who asked so many questions."

"I'm a journalist. It's my job to ask questions."

"I work with computers. I'm a consultant."

"Well I'm sure you do your job well," I said, grinning sheepishly.

"No one else is going to do it for me."

The train's doors opened and closed at four different stations and we were still talking. She wore a white satin blouse beneath her unzipped coat. It glowed when it met the fluorescent light from above.

She was Cuban, born in Santiago, on the southeastern part of the island near the ocean. She had smuggled herself to Nueva York via the Dominican Republic to try something new and see if capitalism was as bad as she'd been taught it was. She'd studied English all her life, learning from books and practicing with an old family of traveling musicians who'd spent some time in the UK of all places. It was no surprise that her English was perfect and followed the rules of grammar to the letter in that *Masterpiece Theater* kind of way.

She got an associate's degree in network management and almost immediately went out on her own. A year later she had a steady list of clients that always managed to pay her bills. But those were all things I didn't care about knowing. Just then our train squeezed into Borough Hall station.

"So what's your name? I mean you gotta tell me since we been talkin' this long."

"Well I don't have to tell you no-thing." she said playfully. *"Pero me llamo Carolina."* She looked out the window and rose to her feet just before the doors opened.

"Is this you?" I asked.

"Yes, nice talking to you."

"Hey, why don't you let me call you?"

She looked at me with a grin, contemplating whether to keep me or throw me back. She knew she had the upper hand as she flashed her perfectly straight and whites.

"No," she uttered matter-of-factly. "But maybe I'll see you again."

I deflated like an untied balloon as she darted through the doors, just as they began to close. Her booty barely avoided a pinch as the thin steel plates came together.

You never saw a woman like that twice on a New York train. Hands pressed to the grimy window, I watched her scurry down the platform like a woman on a mission, leaving me to ponder what was left of my dream deferred. The train started back into the tunnel that led to Manhattan. I was supposed to have gotten off three stops before.

She hovered in my mind for the rest of the trip home. Ms. Carolina would have been the perfect candidate to fill in the blanks, a creature extraordinary enough to position between work and sleep. That was the only thing I needed them for. But there were some, a few, one, who had spilled out of that assigned space, and got in front of everything else. Carolina reminded me of her. And she, that mystery woman from my past, was the one I'd hurt the most.

I played the Mirage interview tapes over and over as I looked for the first quote I was going to use. The piece wasn't due for three weeks but achieving perfection was going to take a lot more time than the average record review, especially when I wanted it to be the one that outdid any and every piece ever written on the artists formerly known as Arbor Day. But the words didn't come and I began to pace the room.

I walked over to the stereo and flipped it on. I'd lost

the remote during my housewarming party the previous summer when somebody threw an incomplete pass and it went out the back window into the building's jungle of a backyard. With the two feet of high grass and broken concrete down there an item like a remote control was never to be found again. Sade sang about love being stronger than pride and I started getting a sensitive feeling I couldn't afford. I switched over to the next disc.

A Tribe Called Quest rhymed about "The Business" through my speakers and my mood got back on its proper course. I sat back down to stare at the brightness of the computer screen. Was I really going to get anything done? The defeatist in me answered in the negative and I decided to get into the streets. There was no point in torturing myself over words that weren't coming. I lit a cigarette. It was a Wednesday night.

There was a Jay-Z show at Irving Plaza, a Q-Tip album release party at the Kit Kat Club, and something else I couldn't precisely remember in the Village. If any of that failed I could always go to the phones and try to get a female on the line, preferably someone who wouldn't be coming over to talk about world issues. Outside of my dreams there were few to none of those. But I could always watch *Road Rules*.

Two hours burned to a crisp as I sat on the couch watching *Rap City*. There wasn't a new video in the day's offerings. For most people, videos were a quaint diversion. But for me they were like the day's ticker tape. I even got to write off cable as a business expense because I considered it "research" when my accountant did my taxes. And it was a legitimate claim. You had to watch all the new videos so you'd have something to talk about with the record company people at all the parties. The escapism of T&A was an added bonus.

But that night, as I looked around my apartment, waiting for something to do to fall into my lap, I realized that I was still living a guppy life in a sea full of sharks and salmon. All my furniture was used and my posters were held up by pushpins instead of frames. The refrigerator coughed and grumbled like a man with bronchitis. While I was living in squalor I imagined that editors like Chad had already made plans for the night, plopping down platinum Amex cards and heading back to their respective cribs with girls that looked like Cameron Diaz.

That was the life I wanted, *sans* the white girls of course. And it wasn't going to come from just one article. My Arbor Day piece would get my foot in the door. But I hoped that my novel, *Caution*, was going to keep me in the room.

I had started writing it when I first came to the Apple. I'd scribbled pages on trains and typed things up when I had a free moment at one of my many temp and freelance jobs. Sometimes I wrote through my lunch breaks, just to get the words out of me and onto a page that would remember them. In my mind it was going to be the book that bent all the rules and changed all the definitions. But the piles of rejection letters had been saying something totally different.

Caution was the story of Delante Caution, a neighborhood fixture in Bankhead Atlanta who got paid to advise the local drug kingpin, a.k.a. the Captain. But the true plot began when the Captain put him in charge of an out-of-town transaction. The deal went bad. And before he knew it Caution found himself trying to save his crew, and more important himself, from rival dealers, cops, and the mother of his child, who was always threatening to leave.

Caution was an imaginary version of all the men I'd wanted to be like when I was a kid, cats who held the corners down and didn't take shit from anyone. If there was a threat, if their respect was compromised, they went for the jugular, and didn't think a thing about it, before it was too late that is.

That book was supposed to be my way out, my escape hatch from the in-the-crossfire war documentary life I was living. It was a chance for me to peel away my required mask, for me to write without the jaded lenses I always wore.

I flipped the TV off and realized that I had to get out

of the house. Set on the Q-Tip party, I changed into a gray Polo sweater and grabbed my coat, hat, and scarf. Just before I reached the door my conscience got the better of me and I turned and looked at the humming and blank computer screen.

I imagined a hand bidding me towards it. I had it in me to stay home and do the work, to get myself one step closer to living the good life before twenty-three. All I had to do was sit down and really try. But that usual voice seductively whispered into my ear. It told me about free liquor and girls open to late-night adult entertainment. I was on the front stoop and down the walkway before I knew it. I stopped again, but this time only to watch the passing silhouettes of my homeward-bound neighbors. Their jobs were over until morning. But mine never seemed to stop.

That was how they got us, how all of us writers and editors and promotions coordinators ended up at the same things all the time. Inside of those little clubs and offices we were representing the thing that meant the most to us, or at least the thing that we really understood. Hip-hop was what our parents had cursed as they snapped our tapes in half after hearing one "muthafucka" too many. When we were in those rooms we were the stars, the ones who got the records first and who told the fans what to buy, who to love and who would survive.

It was an addiction, the worst kind, because the more of it you took in the more of it you needed. And as the years went by your dosage increased to cope with the load. I was on the verge of ODing and it still wasn't doing anything for me. But I kept trying. I kept hoping for another high in dens of more serious junkies.

The Panamanian kids from the building next door were sitting on the stoop in the middle of winter singing along to the Mary J. Blige that blared from their radio. It was a cheap AIWA stereo combo attached to an orange extension cord that ran deep into their building. I waved at them but they didn't notice me in the dark.

I lit my last cigarette on the way to the train and finished it just before I got to the turnstiles. I flicked the butt into a trash receptacle and made my way through the spinning poles to the platform.

I waited for the 4 in the freezing tunnel air. But when the train finally opened its doors the temperature on the heated car was just right. I'd opted for the Q-Tip thing because I knew Jay-Z's would be too much of a hassle to get into. That made it the lesser of the two evils. Then I finally remembered the thing in the Village. My boy Lamar had told me about it the day before. Some little upstart magazine was throwing something at Joe's Pub. It sounded cheesy but the drinks were free before eleven. I quickly hopped off at Brooklyn Bridge and transferred to the 6 local, which let me off right at Joe's front doorstep. Q-Tip would have to see me the next time. Lamar had changed my night and, as it turned out, my life.

A homeless man sat on a park bench in front of the club talking to the small planted tree next to him, a busy Starbucks in the background. I gave him the respect of a "Wassup" but he was too caught up in the conversation to notice. Most people treated the homeless like lepers. I didn't like their funky asses sitting next to me either but I gave them a little something when I could. As broke as I'd been, there were plenty of times when I was half a step away from talking to trees myself.

"Dakotaaaaaaa!" someone yelled in an alto voice. I wasn't surprised to see that it was DeAndra. She was the head publicist at one of the labels but right then I couldn't remember which one. I did remember that she always sent me copies of every new release she had to offer. I had done a couple of articles on some of her artists so we made sure to speak every time we saw each other.

"How you doin', sweetie?" she asked after we did the kiss-each-other's-cheek thing.

"I'm all right, just strugglin' like everybody else."

"Well give me a call and let me know what you're doing," she replied. She cut left toward a crowd of bodies who held the half-consumed drinks of important people. Had I really had something going on she would have tried to talk to me for an hour. I headed toward my favorite place to celebrate another trip to the treacherous island of Manhattan—the bar.

The club looked like a den for vampires. All the overhead lights were red and little chairs and couches surrounded fluorescent-illuminated tables. Cliques had congealed in all four corners of the room. But most folks were crowded over by the trough.

The pseudo players stood in conference along the wall-length bar. They were all terribly overdressed wearing silk shirts, derbies or fedoras, expensive slacks or baggy leather pants, with the shoes to match of course. I knew most of them. But they were barely worthy of a hello. Girls always gave them the attention, particularly the scantily clad ones in search of their next sugar daddy.

The granola girls were there too. They were the easiest to spot because you found them all over. Covered in headwraps and drenched in street-corner oils, they only wore things found at thrift stores and the pricey retro shops in the East Village. They never ate meat or dairy and waited for the day when Afrocentric hip-hop would be back in the forefront. I imagined that in the meantime they spent their nights and mornings praying to shrines dedicated to Lauryn Hill and Erykah Badu.

Then there were the Artists. They headed up the cliques in the corners, conducting their discussions in hushed tones. The looks on their faces screamed that they considered themselves on a higher level than the rest of the crowd. The worst of them had never created a thing in their lives but talked about the process as if it were theoretical physics. The best of them had moved into the mainstream or left the game altogether to do something with more purpose. But they always had friends who could get them in. And they always wanted to be back where all the color was.

I didn't feel like I fit into any of the categories. But I still had folks behind me. You had to have a crew, people in positions that kept you paid and popular. Lamar was my man at *Maintain* and my main homegirl Maya got me into all the fashion and art stuff. She was the only black photographer I knew with those kind of hookups. And I handled the rest. We were three and that was more than enough.

Two pseudo-players made room for me as I nudged my way towards the Asian bartender with the Superman emblem tattooed on the back of his left hand.

"Hennessy straight up," I said as I scanned the bar for familiar faces. He poured the drink quickly, stabbed it with a stirrer, and gave me a look that should have been answered with a tip, especially since the drink was free. But I gave him the peace sign and started to look for a seat.

"D!!!" Lamar yelled. It was a miracle that I heard him

over the new Mobb Deep and Nas cut coming out of the speaker next to the bar. I gave Lamar a nod and once again navigated the silk, leather, and crushed velvet to talk to my man from *Maintain.*

Lamar was the only dude I rolled with when it came to nocturnal operations. He was from upstate and had gone to school at Syracuse, where he got a B.A. in general education and a master's in drinking. He ended up in a detox at twenty-one and started writing while he was in there for three months. Two years later he became associate editor for *Manhole,* one of the smaller rags in the hip-hop family but one that carried just enough pull to get you where you needed to be.

Now, after almost four years, he was one of the two associate music editors at *Maintain.* He didn't do anything noticeable to the pages he worked on. But I had to envy him for the consistent check. He spent every cent of it on clothes, drinks, and the occasional date, when he could get one. And he had memorized all of New York State's laws on housing and tenant eviction, since he rarely paid his rent on time.

"What's goin' on?" I asked.

"Nuthin', just tryin' to talk to these fake-ass girls in here."

He wore a dashiki, one of the many items of clothing that he didn't look right in. It made him look shorter and fatter than he already was. But they'd popped up in a few current videos so he figured they were in.

"What girls you talkin' 'bout?"

"Look over there by the bar."

I turned and spotted her standing next to a guy with a white velvet derby and a silver silk vest. Her hair was done in big dark curls and she wore a powder-blue dress that had a large star attached to it encrusted with glitter. She looked like she'd just come from her prom. But her defective fashion sense aside, she was somewhere above a seven and below a nine, one of Lamar's better targets.

"So what's she talkin' 'bout?"

"Man, I told her I work at *Maintain* and she started askin' me if I could write her a recommendation for a job. I was like damn, can't you even try to butter me up, give me some ass or something before you start askin' me for shit?"

"You should've known better," I said, shaking my head slightly. Lamar wasn't high up enough on the ladder to ask for sexual favors. "She's standing in the player section." Realization slapped him with a leather glove.

"I guess I should've noticed, huh?"

"Yeah," I replied. "It might have saved you time. Least it ain't cost you no money. All the drinks is free."

"That's true. She put away two amaretto sours in the five minutes I was talkin' to her."

I first met Lamar when I was waiting for an interview with the research department at *Maintain*. I'd been in New York for a year and he had just gotten his assistant editor job. He saw me sitting in the lobby on his way out to lunch and noticed my starched shirt and tie and my one pair of slacks. He chuckled, amused that I was going the traditional route.

"You ain't got to keep that top button buttoned up here," he said.

"Why do you say that?" I asked in a tone full of blissful ignorance. I figured going with the good ole Southern boy who wanted to make it in the Big Apple routine would put me over the top.

"Because I got a job here and I can tell you that people who come in here dressed like that don't get hired. Damn, at least take that tie off, fan that collar out a little bit."

I loosened the knot and pulled the satin fabric from around my neck, stuffing it into my breast pocket.

"Now you at least stand a chance," he had said as he went about his business.

I left the interview with the job and the research editor in my back pocket. The kind of white boy who did button his shirts up to the neck, Steven really believed that research was more than the mundane job of checking other people's facts. He cracked the leather at others while he was still tied to the higher-ups' whipping post.

"We'll see you in two weeks," Steven had said through the office door just before I pulled it closed behind me.

"Get it?" Lamar asked as I was on my way to the exit.

"Yeah," I said. We started talking and before I knew it he gave me a pass to a movie screening. After that first night it became a cardinal rule that if I rolled with any-body it would be Lamar. He wasn't smooth with the ladies or with his words on the printed page. But he was my man.

"So what's this party for, anyway?" I semi-yelled to him after taking a sip from my drink.

"I think this is the one-year anniversary for this thing," he said as he drew a rolled blunt from his jacket pocket. "And that's always the reason they celebrate, ain't it? Either that or a million copies sold. Doesn't really matter. Got a light?"

I put a flame to his spliff and he took a deep first pull and passed it to me. I inhaled and the smoke wandered through me like a lost child before dribbling out of my nostrils. Within minutes Dakota Grand was no longer standing at a plastic-coated industry party. I was just a man enjoying the music and admiring the women who looked like they could give my life some meaning.

"Yo man, did you hear?" Lamar asked me a few min-utes later.

"What?" I asked, my mind floating above the bar.

"You ain't read it in the paper?"

"No, man! Look, just tell me what's up."

"Your man Tyrone Fields got jumped last night." I was sober in less than an instant.

"What you mean he got jumped? What Fields do to have somebody whippin' his ass?"

"Nothin'. That's the worst part of it. I heard he did a piece on some no-name group and I guess they didn't like how it turned out 'cause they came all the way from East New York to his office and beat him down in the elevator while one of 'em held the emergency stop button. They broke his jaw, his nose, and two fingers. Plus they gave him two black eyes. Heard he's gonna be working out of his house for a month. Man, the game is gettin' crazy."

"Damn, who told you all this?"

"Monica over at *Manhole*. She said she was upstairs in the office when it all happened."

"Well I guess you can trust her to tell you the truth. She ain't never told me nothing that didn't come out in the wash."

Fields hadn't been the first to take a mopping for something he wrote. There'd been a few sacrificial lambs over the years. The worst one was when Jesse Washington from *Blaze* got a four-man working-over in a conference room for revealing an artist's secret identity. And before that, Masta Killa from Wu-Tang Clan hit Cheo Coker in the face just because he didn't like the artwork on an article he wrote on the group. It had gotten so bad that some writers were giving phony names when they showed up for interviews. We never knew who was going to be next.

Needless to say it bothered me. There we were, journalists, the people standing between the artists, and the white press that didn't give a damn about them. And we were always the ones who ended up in the hospital over a quote some weeded-out rapper didn't remember.

I hadn't expected anything to happen to Fields, though. He had nice things to say about Vanilla Ice's second album. He had even told me a few months before at a party that he was really trying to get lesser-known groups more play at his magazine.

"Hip-hop wasn't born on the radio," he had said to me at a party once. "We need to start actin' like it. The underground is important." But that same underground had flattened him like a pancake. If anybody had tried to do that to me I would've had to show them where I was from. But I returned focus to the issues at hand.

"So what other girls you tryin' to holler at tonight?" I asked him as I scanned the room for my own potential targets.

"All of 'em," he said with a slur. Having ruled out sobriety years before he'd once told me that three drinks was his designated stopping point since detox. Number four was held loosely in his right hand.

"Just stay in your price range," I replied as I drained my glass. "You don't need to be shoppin' for nuthin' you can't afford. Especially not in this room."

"That ain't me," he said with a grin before walking away through a huddle of pseudo-players. I looked around and felt like ice in hot water, destined to dissolve into the life around me. I saw an empty stool at the bar and moved toward it.

"I guess you don't know how to call no more," a voice whined at its signature pitch. When I turned around Stacy was right in front of me, encased in a cloud of co-coa butter and peppermint oil. She was wearing a short black strapless dress with patent-leather platforms. Her light brown hair was cut low as usual. She hadn't changed at all, as if she'd been suspended in time since the last time we'd small-talked earlier in the year.

"I know how to call," I said, pretending that I was really offended. "I just never had the number."

"That's what you said the last time you saw me," she replied, shaking her head. She was the kind of girl who always wanted to be chased. "And I gave it to you."

"I guess I lost it," I said and then paused. "But how you been? What you doin' these days?"

"I'm doin' promotions now. Got my own street team together. We got a few clients. We're really hopin' to do some of the stuff for the next Eve record."

Stacy was one of those New York natives with a nose

for finding a check. This time she was commanding a team of young men and women to paste stickers and posters onto every available surface in the name of up-coming album releases. The last time we talked she had been answering phones for a music video company. And before that she was a manager's assistant. She gave the right kind of smile to the right man and the rent check always cleared.

We'd gone out once. She said she'd call and never did. I actually had called her afterwards and got a recording that said the new number was unpublished. But in public we had to go through the motions like everything was as good as gravy.

"Well it's good to see you doin' your thing," I replied. I gave her a look that wasn't hostile. But it still encour-aged her to scram.

"Well, it was good seeing you again," she said with an earnest smile. Soon after she hovered off towards the granola girls.

There was a part of me that didn't want to see her leave, that wanted to invite her to a cozy dinner at my apartment, drinks overlooking the river at Battery Park in the spring, when it got warmer. There could have been a photograph of us in my wallet, a voice that was happy to hear from me at the beginning and end of each workday, and someone to get used to in bed on the weekends. But that wasn't going to happen under the gelled lights at Joe's Pub, not when the room was filled with men (and women) who had the pockets to give her more, and the resolve to stay in the game, and New York, forever.

I turned around on my stool and stared at my face in the mirror. A bit of a five-o'clock shadow had appeared. Even from a distance I could tell that my eyes were red. But as I sat up I noticed that the man behind the counter wasn't the same one who'd been pouring my drinks for most of the night.

He was tall and slim with big eyes, a face I knew but couldn't place. But his grimace was too familiar not to try. Then, with a belly full of Hennessy and a few buf-falo wings, I figured out who he was: the Shroud.

I was used to him wearing his trademark turban and robes. His most outrageous stunt had been bringing a camel onstage at the MTV Music Awards while he rhymed about being straight from the Sahara. He had been a novelty act, but a pretty successful one. His first single, "Sheik of the Oasis," sampled the "sands from the hourglass" part of the theme from *Days of Our Lives* and made its way onto radio playlists. I had even seen him do a show at the Warehouse while I was in college back home. But the Shroud was short on staying power. The rest of his songs were less than mediocre and before he knew it he got sucked under.

Sitting in front of him years later was like seeing

Hal-Leroy from *Fame* washing dishes in the back of your local carry-out. For a second I thought about saying something, asking what happened to the Shroud, like everyone else probably did. But I knew the story. He'd spent all his money. The record label didn't like his new material, or didn't want to spend the money for him to make any new songs. So he got dropped. Then he couldn't find another deal. And after all hope had faded, after all the shine in his star had tarnished, he'd started checking the help-wanted ads and turned up at Joe's Pub. I kept my mouth shut and drained my glass.

Saying anything, particularly in my drunken state, would have chipped away more of the little dignity he probably had left. I wanted another drink, and a five-spot to give him for a tip. But by that time I didn't have the money to spare for either. The open bar always ended at eleven.

I didn't see Lamar or anyone else I knew for the rest of the night. Instead, I stumbled into a few more petty conversations until there was no one else to talk to. By twelve I was six drinks in and leaning on the bar to stay upright. I sobered slightly during the walk to the subway, even more during the half hour I waited for a train to pull into Astor Place station.

Sitting there, a dozing wino to my right and a transit worker with a soap-and-water spray gun hosing down the floor behind me, I gave myself a telepathic smack for doing it one more time. I'd slid right back into the pit I was trying to climb out of. I could have been back at the house laying the foundation for my Mirage article or even the next literary work of the century. Instead, I was inhaling the smell of industrial-strength cleanser and listening to winter air whistling through the empty tunnels.

A sharp headache formed in the middle of my skull and my eyelids shut to cope with the discomfort. I didn't remember walking the long blocks from the station to my trendy brownstone building on my tree-lined, artsy-people-populated street. I didn't know how I'd climbed the two flights of stairs, or if I'd locked the deadbolt behind me. I woke up that morning facedown on my futon, with dried saliva at both corners of my mouth. I had the urge to try and sleep for the rest of my life. But it passed, like it always did.

The envelopes all looked the same as I fished them out of the mailbox. Four of them were overdue notices from people I couldn't pay. But the fifth was a heavy-papered envelope stamped with a company insignia I didn't recognize right away. But as soon as I opened it I knew it was from one of the fifty publishers to whom I'd sent my excerpt of *Caution*. It was supposed to be my lifeboat out of the madness. But as yet, it wasn't.

Dear Mr. Grand:

We thank you for submitting your query and excerpt of *Caution*, but after careful review we have determined that it does not fit our needs at this particular time. This is in no part a reflection on your creative abilities and we wish you success in your search for another publisher.

Sincerely,

Some Editor

Some Big Major Multimillion-Dollar Conglomerate Publisher

The letter's words chipped away yet another piece of my dream of escaping the grind into the hands of literary glory. Maybe I would never be a published novelist. Maybe I'd spend the rest of my twenties and thirties waking up facedown on metal futons with bent frames, the taste of phlegm with a touch of cognac on my breath.

All the letters had had the same message—polite and encouraging but always without a shred of interest. Maybe a twenty-two-year-old from out-of-town hip-hop writer just didn't stand a chance against a machine that crushed any book query that contained the words "African-American." I frisbeed the letter onto the growing pile of them on the floor next to the futon and flipped through the overdue notices with imaginary concern.

I thought that a book deal would solve everything.

My homegirl Maya always told me that that was unrealistic, that there wasn't enough money in it alone to leave the game. Lamar had agreed with her. But how could they know? Maya worked in lights and lenses. Lamar sat at his desk and barely worked at all. I had to keep believing, even if it felt like it was in vain.

Charged by frustration, I walked over to the desk and took a seat. My laptop was already on. I gathered my notes and prepared to write my first draft of the Mirage piece. The sunlight squeezed through my matchstick blinds and turned my living room a pretty orange color that I barely noticed.

A half hour later I brewed coffee and began to transcribe my interview tapes. Two hours after that I had pulled twelve of the best quotes. Then I went online and pulled up everything else I could find about Mirage. Within the next three days I called and interviewed the writers who wrote those other pieces.

And in four days the first draft was written, along with three record reviews and the artist profile that was due that week. I put more effort into the opening paragraph than I had in my last five features combined. It was on the fifth day that I decided to rest.

Erica Kane's face had to be at least 50 percent plastic. It looked too artificial to be fully human. She'd been doing her best to look thirty for half my life and she had to be running out of actual face to lift. *All My Children* was my way of treating myself to a day off. Off days were relatively frequent, the twenty-four-hour periods I spent shirking assignments in favor of doing whatever I wanted. They were usually Wednesdays. But a free day in the middle of the week always made Tuesday and Thursday even more hectic.

Outside, freezing rain came down from the sky in suitcases. The sound of ice crystals bouncing off the cars on the street below was somehow soothing. My mama had introduced me to the soap-opera world of Pine Valley when I was a kid during the Christmas holidays. I didn't have to go to school and she took her vacation to be with me. Now, nearly two decades later, I was semiaddicted. But I still didn't get why millions of women dedicated their lives to that show. But then again, anyone watching network TV at one in the afternoon clearly didn't have anything else better to do. I turned the channel to BET. That was when the phone rang.

"Is this Dakota Grand," the voice asked in a cautious and nonthreatening tone. Had to be a bill collector.

"Yeah. And who's this?"

"My name is Todd Markewitz. I'm an editorial assistant at W. L. Pressman Publishing." The fine hairs on the back of my neck stood erect.

"Uh, I read your excerpt of *Caution,* in the slush pile here. The slush pile is—"

"I'm familiar with what a slush pile is," I responded as if offended. Actually, I was offended. I knew everything there was to know about the publishing game. In a year and a half it seemed as if I'd almost read every book on the subject.

"Well I think it's excellent and I want to pass it on to my boss, Mark Murphy, one of the associate editors. I think he might be interested in publishing it here. Would you be interested? Or have you already found a publisher?"

"Yeah, umm no. I mean, please pass it on. I really hope that he's interested." I couldn't put up my cool facade fast enough.

"That's good," he said plainly. "I'll get it to him and see what he says. Hopefully you'll hear back from me in a few days or so."

"All right," I replied.

"Nice talking to you and I hope that we get to work together."

"Same here, peace," I said as I hung up the phone.

The warm sticky feeling started in my toes and worked its way up through my chest. There was hope, hope that had come just one day after my twentieth rejection. And they had Hal call me. They didn't send a letter or an e-mail. They picked up the phone and called. And after a call like that I wasn't just a writer anymore. I was on my way to being an *author*, just like all the ones who lived out in Vermont with their 2.5 kids, the Benz, and the station wagon. I was about to be like them, without the gray hair and sweater-and-slack combos.

But I didn't jump up and down. I didn't immediately call Lamar or Maya to spread the news. An amateur would have done that, dancing around over something that wasn't even definite. Instead I sat on the couch and stared blankly at my screen saver across the room. The words "It'll Happen" ran across the black screen. And at that moment I really believed them. I'd tell everyone else when it was more solid. I just wanted to spend the rest of the day carrying that warmth. But as I thought further I realized that it would have been better to share the warmth with someone else, literally. There was only one girl in my current stable and I already knew the number by heart.

"Hello?" Jen responded in a perky but skeptical tone.

"I got somethin' to tell you."

"Who is this?"

"I'm really mad you don't know my voice."

"Oh, well why should I, D? It's not like I hear it all that often."

"Look, don't be mad. I'm just out here trying to do my

thing." She gave me two huffs and a puff. "But look, can you just hold back from being mad at me for like two seconds?"

"One . . . two, now I'm mad again. You know, I got a lot of papers to grade tonight." She was pretty convincing as the woman fed up with my flakiness. But I knew it wasn't going to take much to get around her little tantrum.

"I got a deal for my book." There was a long pause. She was melting.

"Oh, congratulations, sweetie!" she exploded, as if I hadn't stood her up two consecutive weekends in a row. "You know you gotta tell me all about it."

"Well actually I wanted to know if you wanted to celebrate with me, go out and get something to eat."

"Ohhhh, I'm sorry, but like I said, you caught me when I got a stack of papers to grade. And I gotta give my kids a test tomorrow."

Jennifer Blackmon was the only number I had to dial and I still treated her terribly. I called when I felt like it and returned her calls even less frequently. She taught sixth grade at P.S. something or another over in Flatbush. And she was a sizzler, an Erykah Badu–like face on Angela Bassett's body. She could have been the poster girl for any gym in town, or the lead sex object in my Jay-Z video.

I met her at the Noreaga record release party. She was

there at the bar with her girlfriend, dressed like she was on her way to church, or maybe a job interview. I had on a T-shirt, jeans, and boots, and I bought her a drink and told her exactly what she wanted to hear. That was how it started.

"Come on," I said, dropping my voice an octave. "You can grade them later."

"No I can't. I gotta get my final grades in. The quarter's over next week."

"Well I can't stop the children from getting their education, now can I?" The "I really-don't-want-to-mess-up-your-job" card seemed like a good one to play.

"Well." She paused, her journey to the Dark Side close to completion. "When I think about it it isn't gonna take me all night. I'm about halfway done. Why don't you come by around eleven?" Eleven was too late for any kind of eating. All I would need was a condom and a story, both of which I kept in ample supply.

"Are you sure? I mean I don't want you to not get your grades in."

"It's okay. I'll have everything all done by the time you get here."

"Well all right then eleven it is."

"I'll see you then."

"All right then."

"And D?"

"What?"

"I'm really proud of you."

"Thanks," I said, wearing Satan's smile.

■ ■ ■

I WASN'T GOING to brag about my call from Pressman but I had to tell somebody. And Maya was the opposite choice. There were a million folks who swore that we were a couple. But that just wasn't the way that she and I got down. Maybe we were too much alike, both of us searching for unrealistic salvation from our respective hells.

"Don't pop the champagne just yet," Maya said just before taking a sip from the Merlot in her glass. "I mean I been telling you that book was good since you started writing it. But until the ink is on the page just remember that people are good at talking and they're good at doing their best, until they come up short."

"I see I just can't get no love from you," I said. "But I wouldn't expect much more from a pointy-eared Vulcan anyway." I rubbed the taste of Hennessy against the roof of my mouth. "But I'm just glad you invited me out here to celebrate."

"Well since I'm one of the few people you let be your friend in this city I figured the least I could do was buy you a few drinks. We haven't hung out in a while and besides I'm not afraid to admit that I'm really happy for little brother. I'm sure they'll make you an offer."

I'd met her at the bar at the *Blaze Online* launch party, a half hour before a fight broke out on the dance floor to the sounds of "Superthug." I was trying to get the number of a model/video "actress" and she was sitting next to me at the bar talking to one of the only black label execs from Sony. I surprisingly ended up with the girl's digits and Maya got his business card. Ten minutes later we ended up talking to each other.

"It's terrible isn't it, this whole scene?" she had asked while staring at her reflection in the mirror behind the bar. Her almond face was garnished with a cute dusting of freckles and her Prada bag hadn't come off of a vendor's table outside of the Manhattan Mall.

"Yeah, but it's the only one I know how to play," I had replied. "And I'm nowhere near being tired of it either."

"You'll get tired of it," she had said glumly as she turned to me, her long auburn hair pinned up like a Japanese geisha girl's. "Everybody gets tired of it."

As a photographer her world was a little different from mine, more white people, more gay people, more gay white people. She was that bourgie black girl who didn't get black friends until after college. But I liked the way she put her thing down. And since she was a little older she had the New York state of mind down pat. For her it was all about the work, magazine covers, commercial layouts, the occasional album cover, whatever it took to get her where she wanted to go. She owned some rental property down in Florida and made her rent sleeping. I needed someone like that around me, particularly when almost everyone else was a gang of underachievers. Three weeks after we met I let her read *Caution*. Now, a year later, we were drinking to my potential deal in a Brooklyn Heights bar.

"Shouldn't you be at some little hoochie's house tonight?" she said before draining her glass.

"Oh don't you worry, I will be, right after I leave here." My watch said it was 11:05. "Supposed to be there now but I'll let her sweat for a while." Maya shook her head.

"You shouldn't treat them like pets. You know? Keeping them on leashes."

"I don't."

"Yes, you do."

"No, I don't. I don't lie to nobody. Besides, I can't let nobody get too close. At least not now. I'd get pimped that way."

"Is that you talking or somebody else?"

"What's that supposed to mean?"

"Sometimes I wonder if you're two different people in one body, especially when I remember how you were with Xi—"

"Hey, that was another lifetime," I interjected. "And I learned from that. That ain't the way I need to go."

"So I guess you'd rather do the Ayanna thing?"

"The Ayanna thing?"

"Forgotten her already?"

"No," I replied even though I almost had. "But what did I do wrong to her?"

"You met her in the pressroom at that Fubu fashion show, told her how intelligent and special you thought she was, and got her over to your house for the night."

"So?"

"Then you slept with her, woke her up at six in the morning, and threw her out because you said you had to go to work early. The only thing you do at six in the morning is roll over, maybe adjust your pillow."

"Hey, that was her fault for fuckin' me *before* the first date. Everybody knows I don't like havin' girls hangin' around the crib."

"You can play the innocent role or you can admit that you knew that you could get over on her and had no shame in doing whatever it took to get in her pants."

"I really don't think she's out there somewhere heart-broken over it. She just doesn't call me anymore."

"Can you blame her? Doing stuff like that doesn't help anything. It only contributes to the problem."

"And what problem is that?"

"Why black men and women can't get along."

I chuckled.

"I'm not even trying to hear this from you. You done fucked with more white boys than Diana Ross." The almond tone on her face went flush. She hadn't expected me to go that deep into the skeleton closet.

"We're not talking about me," she said, offended. But her anger only lasted for a second or two. "And besides, I was done with white guys way before I even met you. I went to a white school, grew up on the East Side. I had a serious lack of exposure. But as far as you're concerned, I'm just saying that women aren't disposable, so you shouldn't treat them that way."

"All right, Maya," I said with a sigh.

"You know, one of these days you're due to meet a woman who you care about. I just hope she doesn't throw you away."

"Well, I'll deal with that when it comes," I said arrogantly. Her prediction was nowhere in my current deck of cards.

"I hope you do," she said. She took a brief pause. "So which one is it tonight?"

"Jen."

"The teacher?"

"Yeah."

"Well, have a good time."

"You know I will," I said as I looked at my watch

again. "Look, I gotta get out of here." I rose from the table and threw my coat on. "I'll call you tomorrow."

"Be safe," she said maternally just before I pushed myself out onto the icy chill coming off of the river. I stopped for a moment to look at the skyline across the Promenade. The Empire State was lit in Christmas colors. The city always looked peaceful from a distance.

I grinned when I saw an empty cab on the corner and I jogged in its direction. But it pulled off before I got there. It took three more tries on three different blocks before I finally found the pleather comfort of a rear passenger seat. I was at Jen's in under ten minutes, thirty minutes behind schedule. I got out of the cab and walked towards the building.

I rang the downstairs buzzer twice before I realized that the front door had been left open. Just past the foyer, a standing sign in Magic Marker announced that the elevator was broken, leaving me with a three-flight walkup. The elevator in her building only worked for two-week intervals. I unzipped my coat and began the climb.

The echo of multiple gunshots filtered through the window above the stairwell. I passed several doors on the way up, one that barely restrained the thumping bass of reggae and another the smell of incense and cooked food. Her door, the last on the hallway, was cracked, a deep red light glowing behind it.

I gave the door a slight tap and it glided open. She was sitting in the chair next to her bed, which she had strangely placed close to the door. She was wearing a short robe with obviously very little underneath, her shiny legs crossed.

"Why do you always have to be late? I've been sitting here for a half an hour." Her doll-like face wrinkled in disgust.

Her efficiency was small, with barely enough room for the bed, sofa, and recliner it contained. The refrigerator against the far wall was covered with student artwork but the beige walls were totally bare. If those little kids only knew what their teacher and I were going to do before she came to work in the morning.

"My meeting ran late," I said. "I'm sorry." I gave her an honest look that said that I meant it. She stood up and walked over to me.

"Well take your coat off. You are staying, aren't you?" She smiled as I peeled out of my leather and she hung it up in the closet that separated the bedroom from the kitchen.

"Yeah, we supposed to be celebratin', right?" She gave me a Colgate smile and reached over to hug me. I felt the outline of her body as I pulled her against me.

"So you gotta tell me all about it," she said.

"There's not that much to tell," I replied. "I mean some

kid found the manuscript in a pile and read it. He passed it to his boss and now they want to sign me." Sure, it was a lie, but closer to the truth than I usually came with her.

"Well, you don't seem excited about it."

"I'm more excited about seeing you," I said. I kissed her on the forehead first and she stood on her toes so her lips could reach my mouth. She kissed me deeply and then put her feet back flat on the floor.

While she was of a far higher grade than industry rats, Jen had another problem that kept me on the periphery. If she liked me, the kind of like that went beyond what we'd done in our respective bedrooms, then she'd always want me there, always want the flowers, always want the walks in Prospect Park, always want me on her arm at some friend's Tupperware party out in Queens. There was a responsibility that came with the feelings. And I didn't think I could deal with it, not with her. The magnetism wasn't strong enough to pull me in. But I also couldn't tell her the truth: that in too many ways she was nothing more than a release.

If I actually told her that she'd probably block my number, put the word out on the streets that I was an asshole, jeopardizing my edibly clean reputation, and effectively shut down my operation. So I kept her somewhere in between, in a place where neither of us could *really* hurt the other.

"Close your eyes," she said. I obeyed and listened to her hit the light switch and light several candles. Then there was the shuffling of fabric.

"I missed you," she said.

"I missed you too," I replied out of courtesy.

"Now open your eyes."

Her naked body glowed in the candlelight as she stood a few feet in front of me. Her thick nipples stood at attention on grapefruit-sized breasts. Her stomach was a little flabby but I couldn't tell whenever I saw her laying on her back, with a new morning's sunlight softly covering her like a blanket. Neither of us spoke.

My shoes and socks were abandoned immediately as I was almost too eager to get it going. We kissed again, my arms slithering around her waist to grip her buttocks. She pulled me towards the bed, where our difference in height didn't matter.

My shirt went over my head and soon went sailing towards the floor. I kept my pants on as my tongue traced the outline of her torso, the flesh on her thighs. The skin on her fingers and toes alike was taut and moist. From there I didn't know where to go. But I knew where she wanted me to end up. The song in my mind was Prince's "International Lover." I became liquid as I wrapped around and slid into her. She squirmed and moaned, murmuring my name and several expletives. Each word, each move she made gave me more strength, more control.

"I really missed you," she said in the throes. The words made me nervous. It was time to close it out. Our faces scrunched with pleasure, and she let out a sound that might have stirred the neighbors in another part of Brooklyn. I exploded and crashed on top of her, sweat gluing us together like facing pages in a book.

After two flicks of a lighter cigarette smoke choked the aroma of incense in the air. I pulled deeply and ex- pelled a cloud that appeared to twist into a large ques- tion mark above the bed before dissipating. Minutes later she extinguished her half-finished square in the ashtray and curled up like a kitten, her semicircle of a rear down and to the right of me.

A draft pierced through the cracked window on the other side of the room. My hunger had been quenched. But as her breathing fell into a snore I almost forgot what had brought me there. I should have left. Instead I just laid there, staring at the ceiling through two more cigarettes until I drifted off.

I woke up just before dawn, got dressed, and slithered onto Flatbush Avenue with the stealth of a ninja. Inside the train station I scanned the billboards on the platform for anything new to consume. But I only saw repeated copies of a cigarette ad some couple had vandalized with a Magic Markered heart, their names in the middle. They'd tagged every board on the platform with the same insignia.

Love was not simple. The job made my life hard enough. I didn't *need* anything else to complicate it. The D train rushed in just as the thought completed itself. I turned up the Outkast in my headphones to thwart any further distractions.

■   ■   ■

I WOKE UP to the squawking of two ravens in the tree outside of my bedroom window. Tyra Banks grinned at me as she stood half naked and pinned to the wall that I was facing. I peered out of the framed glass just in time to see the huge birds flapping off, their job now done. I was still fully dressed and Jen had left an early-morning message on my voice mail saying how upset she was that I had left in the middle of the night, that I hadn't locked the door behind me. I erased it.

I had a record review to finish that I hoped would give me enough money to make the rent at the end of the month. I got up and traveled three paces to the beanbag chair, where I got the CD in question out of my bag and dropped it into the changer.

I'd heard the drum line before. I could tell the producer's sampling wasn't timed correctly and the rapper's delivery didn't move me. I scanned through six more songs and found the same symptoms on each and every one. I walked over to the pad on the kitchen counter and scribbled down a few notes before switching discs to James Brown's greatest hits. "The Big Payback" flooded through the speakers.

I started with a little yoga and jumping jacks, followed by crunches, dips, and push-ups. Then I cooled down with orange juice, BET, and a Newport. I wrote the piece quickly, hammering 250 words into an e-mail and sending it off with an invoice attached. The words "Your mail has been sent" produced a deep exhale and a final pull from my square just as James and his band brought the track to a close.

I had a few runs to make in Brooklyn. I needed toilet paper. There were packages to mail at the post office. Chicken breasts were on sale at the Pathmark. Then it was off to the city, where $500 in checks was waiting to be picked up at three different receptionists' desks. When I stepped out I noticed that the sky was a medium gray, a cheerful color for New York winters. I moved from place to place going over the previous day's events. I wondered how far this Mark Murphy was into the *Caution* manuscript, if Todd was putting good words in at every available moment. My subconscious wandered other places but reality hit me on the corner of 28th and Third Avenue.

I stopped at a bodega and picked up the *Daily News* to check the afternoon headlines. Page two caught my attention immediately. The headline read: "Rap Journalist Attacked in Club Bathroom." I had to read it twice just to make sure my mind wasn't April-fooling me.

The story went on to explain how Walt Wilson II, known in the rap magazine world as WWII, had been hospitalized for a concussion and broken ribs after being attacked in the bathroom of the Tunnel nightclub in lower Manhattan.

The attack was rumored to be related to a record review he had written which had trashed the latest album from the rap group Massive Onslaught. There had been no witnesses other than Wilson himself, who had seen nothing since he was first hit from behind at a urinal and could identify no one. No charges had been filed nor arrests made.

As I inhaled the trail of incense coming from behind the immigrant East Indian–clerked counter, I was surprised that another incident had happened so soon, and to someone closer to home. I'd worked with Wilson when I was in research at *Maintain*. Sure there had been plenty of times where I'd wished that someone would put a straight jab to his crooked face. But giving someone a beatdown while they were taking a piss was pretty gangster.

I always saw Wilson as one of those Ivy League Negroes who felt like his degree made him better than the rest of us, even though he never met deadlines and still used slang from the '80s. But for the moment I let that go. The Wilson beating meant that there had been two attacks in a few days. This one had been reported in the press. That was something to worry about.

I tossed the paper into a trash basket at the corner of Third and 33rd as I headed toward the 6 train. A film-developing shop with the grimiest windows I'd ever seen announced a double-prints-for-a-single-price sale. A baby cried frantically in a passing stroller on the opposite side of the street. I turned left on 33rd and stopped at the corner where *MOOD* magazine used to be.

I paused and looked at the building's cornerstone and thought about the scores of calls I had made there in hopes of getting to write a profile or a record review. But like at so many other places all I got were evil voice-mail greetings and apathetic return calls encouraging me to send in article ideas with my clips. I always sent them and they always vanished into *MOOD's* Bermuda Triangle. I smiled the day they folded.

Stuck in the flashback I barely felt it when someone tapped me on my shoulder. I did a 180 to see Allen Reeves's face hovering a few inches above my head. His skinny frame was wrapped in a tweed overcoat with a matching turtleneck and scarf underneath.

"Yo waasup Allen? How you doin' man?"

"Cool brother, what's your name again? I used to always see you at *Maintain* a while back. What you doin' now?"

"I just been writin' man, still tryin' to get up there wit' you."

A statement like that was usually empty flattery for the sake of being polite. But in Reeves's case it didn't even bother me that he didn't remember who I was. He was one of the ones who laid the groundwork, who back in the day had written pieces for the love. He took hip-hop journalism to heavy hitters like *The New Yorker* and *Vanity Fair*. He spoke at colleges, was guaranteed to be a panelist at any given hip-hop forum. He was rumored to be working on screenplays and living in a remodeled brownstone he owned. Reeves was the Louis Armstrong of the game, the man I had to read whenever I saw his byline.

"I'm not anyone to be like," he said plainly as the light before us turned green. But neither of us moved to cross. "You have to choose your own path." I just wanted him to say that he had read one thing I'd done, for him to acknowledge me for one small thing he might have seen, even if he was just reading *Maintain* and *Fluff* in the bathroom.

"Yeah man, I been writin' a lot," I said clumsily. "Doin' stuff for *Maintain* and *Fluff*. I'm even workin' on this piece for the cover of—"

"So what are you *reading* now?" He interjected the words so smoothly that my forced pause felt natural.

"Huh?" It was far from the response I'd expected.

"Any writer has to read." The stoplight had switched from red to green twice by then.

"Well I read *Black Boy* a little while ago and I always read—"

"Let me guess. *The Source, Maintain,* hip-hop stuff, right? . . ."

"Yeah, but . . ."

"Before you become a writer you have to know what a writer does. You need to read before you type one word. You young brothers need to learn that. That's my advice."

He flashed what was less than a good-luck grin and walked away so fast that I thought he was being timed. I stood there for more than a few moments trying to figure out how a basic conversation had turned into a snub from one of the only writers I respected. If he had to leave he could have said that he didn't have time to talk. He could have referenced whatever it was that I'd done to make him dis me like that. My ego was face first against the concrete in front of me. He had a lotta nerve. But I would have my time. And when my time came, I wouldn't forget our little incident at 33rd and Park.

I flicked the butt from my Newport into the bushes

before I entered my building. The stairwell seemed longer than usual, as did the turn of the lock that granted me entrance to Apartment 2C. I tossed my backpack on the beanbag in the corner and plopped myself on the futon next to the answering machine.

There were three messages. The first one was from my mother.

"Hello son," she said in a tone that meant she was mad at me. "When was the last time you called your mother? It's bad enough you're up there runnin' the streets with all those rappers and everybody that does all those drugs. I read about one of 'em getting arrested the other day. But anyway, I just called because I knew you wouldn't. Call me back and at least let me know that you're alive." She hung up.

Mama had been less than supportive about my career choice, particularly since I'd left school (with three semesters remaining) to fully pursue it. She remembered the times I'd called her for money much more often than the packages I sent her with magazine clips and thank-you cards. In her mind, if I wasn't going to do it her way it was the highway, as far as getting her approval was concerned. Maybe if I had gone to grad school, got an editorial job at a publishing company. That would have floated her boat just fine. But I had to be in the trenches, doing the work of covering the world the

Times and *Ebony* and everyone else treated like it didn't even exist.

But how she felt ate away at me a lot of the time, especially when I got a utility cutoff notice or when somebody's accountant told me it would take eight weeks for me to get paid. I had done far better than Pop. But still, I wasn't making my hardworking, nonsmoking, churchgoing single mother proud, like all black boys want to do by the time they become men.

The second message was from Lamar. There was another party that night, but I wasn't interested in going. I had to play the third message back three times before I believed it. It was 9–9.

"Yo son, this is 9–9, one half of what used to be Arbor Day before that muthafucka lost his mind. But anyway, I heard you was doin' a piece on Mirage and wanted to talk to you about it, make sure my side of the story got told right."

Everyone in the industry knew that it might have been easier to get an interview with Michael Jackson than 9–9. He was notorious for showing up at appointments six hours late and giving one-word answers until writers threw their recorders against the wall in frustration. I'd heard that once he'd even gone as far as sending his younger brother (who looked a lot like him) to do interviews he wasn't in the mood for. Now, the man who wouldn't talk to anyone about what happened with Arbor Day wanted in on my story. I replayed the message one final time and copied the number he'd left into my address book. It took me twenty minutes to get the courage to dial and when I did it rang nearly ten times before he picked up, the sounds of voices and movement in the background.

"Yeah," he answered, as if annoyed.

"Yo 9, this is Dakota Grand," I yelled into the receiver.

"Tomorrow, two p.m. at the label office." A dial tone followed. But I kept the receiver to my ear, hoping that he might somehow return to say something else. But I soon forced my thumb against the off button.

I checked the messages. All of a sudden everyone wanted me to go out. Maya called me during *MTV Jams* to ask if I wanted to go with her to the listening party for the new DMX album. She said she knew his stylist and that if I went I might be able to get an interview out of it. I'd interviewed him before and I knew in my heart that I couldn't go out. I had to prepare.

I sat in silence with the TV on mute. I'd grabbed a ballpoint pen and the pad from the kitchen to make a long list of potential questions for the other half of what had been Arbor Day. Mirage had been the brighter side and I would now probe into the darkness that 9 had made so prominent in his four albums' worth of lyrics.

But as I wrote I thought about Mama again, about

how even if I called her then and there she still wouldn't appreciate what I was doing with my life. To her 9–9 was two numbers with a dash in the middle, nothing more. She had wanted me to be a professor or a lawyer or a newspaper reporter, something that made me wear a suit and keep my hair cut short. What I did wasn't good enough to share with her friends in church or to Mr. and Mrs. Murphy across the street from our house.

My mother, Doris to everyone else, spent most of my childhood telling me how destined I was to succeed. She said it was why I had to come in early, why I couldn't run the streets with my boys from around the way. But when I'd made my choice it hadn't been the right one, for her. More than anything I'd wanted her to be proud, to know that what I did was important, that it stood for something, even if I wasn't sure of what it was.

There were no more calls for the rest of the night. I dozed off in the middle of an *ER* rerun and woke up at midnight with a terrible case of the munchies. Two PBJs and a shot of milk easily took care of it. I went back to sleep an hour later and fell into a dream that was more out of the ordinary than usual.

I was in a laundromat wearing a three-piece suit and a pair of patent-leather shoes. WWII was laid flat across the folding table next to me while he told me that he didn't understand why he had gotten his ass whipped. Scars cut deep into his face. Then Fields walked in with two fine halter-topped and tennis-skirted females, one on each arm. The only thing was that his left hand was completely missing. I watched him as he leaned over to one of the girls and whispered, "See that dude over there." He pointed to me and the caramel-skinned one with the globelike ass nodded and grinned. "If he only knew." Fields laughed loudly, his voice echoing throughout the area like it was a bathroom. Then it all faded to black and I sprung into an upright position on the futon.

It was 8 a.m. and this time there was nothing to welcome me back to the world but a few dark clouds in the sky outside of my window. As each second passed the dream became more and more remote. I walked towards the kitchen sluggishly, my muscles wound around each other like thread on a spool. By the time I got there I remembered next to nothing. I had a sip of OJ and then went back to the living-room floor to stretch. Then I smoked half a cigarette before I started my workout. I cooled down with a cup of coffee and thought of my plan for the day, almost forgetting about my interview with 9. But it flooded back when I glanced at the ragged sheets of questions I'd left on the coffee table.

I threw on a pair of sweatpants and a fleece and jogged down to the Time Bagel Café on Atlantic for pancakes and sausage. I picked over my breakfast as I stared through the front window. Outside, people moved back and forth like drones in a hive. I was hidden behind glass, protected from their daily grind. But I always had to deal with my own.

On the way my mind spilled over with images of 9–9 and questions about why he had set things up this way. Was I walking into some sort of an ambush? Or would a man known for bad interviews give me a hard time just for his own twisted amusement? I had no idea. But he was the missing piece in the story I knew would change my life. I also knew that he in turn wanted something as well. I was anxious to find out what it was.

Arbor Day's breakup hadn't been a falling-out over rumors or money. As far as we could tell there wasn't anything juicy about it at all. It was supposed to be a mutual business decision. But Mirage had said plenty to the contrary in my interview with him.

All *we*, the media, knew was that on a Thursday night the two did a show to a packed house at DC's 9:30 Club. They left the club in the same car, as always, and rode off into the night. Then the next morning Vertigo Records faxed one-paragraph press releases to everybody with a byline that said the group was finished. I'd read longer collection notices. But there wasn't a doubt in our collective mind that it was for real. When Lamar called me with the news he sounded like he was fighting the urge to go into a crying fit.

I didn't want to believe it either. They had been together too long, made too many songs that I worshiped, done too many concerts. I was waiting for some twist ending, a prank they'd pulled on the whole industry. But as I crossed the threshold at their label's building on 59th Street across from the CompUSA where Lamar's brother worked and stole things in his spare time, I knew that such fairy-tale endings were only in books.

An intricate marble elevator carried me to the eighth floor. The elevator doors parted cleanly and quietly and I gave a quick wave to Alondria Mendez, the receptionist, who used to be the receptionist at *Maintain* before she got fired for repeatedly calling Busta Rhymes's cell phone number after buying it for $50 from an ambitious intern. She let me pass with a smile, remembering that I had helped her carry her little box of belongings down to a cab just before the upstairs security goons were sent to *walk* her out.

Alondria's long blue nails made an impression against the jet-black phone she held to her ear as I passed. Sheila, Vertigo's publicity head, had an office that was the fourth one on the right. The floor was quiet. I assumed the interns were probably out on errands, buying lunch or baby-sitting one of the artists, maybe even rolling joints in one of the conference rooms. But Sheila herself, all five feet two of her, was already in her doorway, her face expressionless, as it always was.

Sheila was never very pleasant to be around. She always seemed like she was on the verge of a suicide attempt. But keeping artists clean in the eyes of the media could do that to you. We shook hands for the millionth time. Her blondish-brown cornrows matched her fair skin and aquiline features almost perfectly.

"He'll see you now," she said, as if she and Alondria out front had switched places. She motioned me to follow her to the conference-room door, where she stopped abruptly. The threshold was her predetermined cutoff. She knocked twice, cracked the door, and then vanished without a trace.

The sound of coughing came through the doorway as I entered, not knowing if I was ready for what was on the other side. Before I entered I noticed that I was going into the bigger conference room of the two on the floor, the one I'd never been in. This was it. I turned the knob and pushed the door open.

Arthur Ballard, a.k.a. 9–9, sat at the end of a long shiny black table that practically stretched the length of the whole room. On the left there were six chairs in a row facing a huge entertainment center. On the right was a huge photo of the company's founder and CEO, who Maya had once told me enjoyed the company of underage boys at his home in Westchester.

9 coughed again as he sat slouched against the chair's

leather back. His clothes, a plain hooded sweatshirt and a pair of baggy jeans, like Mirage's before him, looked as if they'd been slept in.

"So what'd he tell you?" he asked in a low muttering tone.

"Who?"

"Don't act stupid, muthafucka," he exploded. "You know what I'm here for!"

He drew a Newport, his last, from the crumpled pack on the table, and softly ran it across his lips before lighting. My tape was rolling.

"He said that when y'all started sellin' records you grew apart, that you wanted to be a star and he just wanted to be a musician. He said that was why y'all broke up."

"Is that what that muthafucka said?"

"For the most part."

"What the fuck do you mean for the most part? I ain't ask you to come here and give me a fuckin' summary. I want to know what he said. I want to know everything."

As a journalist I was supposed to check my ego at the door and keep doing whatever it took to keep him talking. But being yelled at wasn't something I dealt with well, even if it was from one of my favorite rappers of all time. I took a deep breath before replying. The smell of smoke set off my own craving for nicotine. But I had left my squares at home on the kitchen counter.

"We mostly talked about the new album," I replied.

"Really," he asked almost excitedly. "How is it?"

"It's really good." I wanted to tell him it was better than anything they had ever done together. But I knew better.

"You know when Mike first started making beats he was terrible. I used to tell him that he could make 'Happy Birthday' sound fucked up." He chuckled at his own joke.

"But you know time passed and it was like he'd do things with a sampler and a keyboard I didn't think was possible. I mean . . . he got better than me. Sometimes I didn't even feel like I needed to be in there with him."

"So you're saying that you intentionally started to move away so that he could do the production work?"

"Hell, fuck no!" he exploded before taking another deep drag from his cigarette. He paused for a moment to file through the memories. "I mean . . . he'd do whole songs behind my back and then bring me in just to put vocals on them. That wasn't the way we started. That was when I knew we wasn't a group no more. We didn't used to work like that. After that I started doing the movie stuff. I wanted him to have his way. He's my boy and when it came to the group I wanted him to be happy. I mean we started makin' music as friends. If my friend wants to do more on the music then I just gotta do more somewhere else. But it wasn't about the group. He was tearin' his whole world down."

"What do you mean by tearing his whole world down?"

"He started lyin' to his wife about real dumb shit. He'd say he had a show to do in Oakland when he'd really be right across town at the studio. He shut himself off from everybody. Didn't even return his mom's calls sometimes. I don't think he ever slept. He was lacing his weed with angel dust, taking those mushrooms and shit. My boy Damien said that he made him drive around the neighborhood, past the same three streets over and over again for like an hour. And that was like two days ago."

"Did you talk to him about it?"

"Whenever I tried to talk to him he told me I was trippin', that I didn't know him or what he was trying to do. He said I didn't care about Arbor Day no more, that I was out tryin' to be a star, that I didn't care about the music. And when he said that I was through. There I was, the one who showed him how to do everything, and he wanted to say I didn't care. I told him it was over, in the studio, right when we were mixin' down this song. He just gave me this real crazy look, then he went back to looking at the mixing board like I hadn't said nothin'."

If the tape hadn't been there I wouldn't have been able to write it down. Not only was Arbor Day over but it looked like my favorite one of the famous pair seemed like he was on his way to the loony bin. I kept my composure and got everything I could on tape. One more question would be enough.

"So why do you want people to know about all of this?" I asked in my Ed Bradleyesque baritone.

" 'Cuz I want the fans to know the truth. Just 'cuz I smoke a lot of weed and mess with a lot of bitches don't mean that I don't tell the truth. People twist shit up, make the good guys into the bad guys when we all just people. And I can't stand for that."

"But this article isn't just about you. Arbor Day is two people, two people with two different views."

"My ass it is! I'm half of everything the world knows him for. And if I don't make a solo album or be in another movie, I want people to know that I left because there wasn't nothin' to stay for. No more gas in the tank. We started out just wantin' to make somethin' different, give the world a new sound. And we did. Millions of people know who we is. I want Mike to remember that when he reads this shit."

He dropped his cigarette on the carpeted floor and rubbed it out with his boot. Then he slumped back in the chair as if some possessing spirit had departed. The honesty in his eyes was replaced by the arrogance I'd expected, the attitude that had once reduced Lamar's potential cover story interview to six sentences' worth of quotes he barely swelled into a 500-word profile.

"That it?" he asked, seeming annoyed that I was still sitting there.

"Yeah," I replied. He rose slowly and dragged himself and his Polo bubble coat out of the conference room. I pushed stop and rewound the tape. Like at my Mirage interview I hoped that everything I'd heard was actually on there, that the story others had failed to get was now in my possession.

"So did you get anything from him?" Lamar asked with a mouthful of grilled chicken salad crunching between his words.

"He gave me a better ten minutes than I expected. He really broke it all down for me."

"He said that much? What'd he say?"

"I'll let you hear the tape when I'm done with it," I replied. I wasn't in the mood to retell the whole story, particularly since I was still hating the end of it.

"He didn't give me shit when I talked to him," Lamar replied, with a tinge of jealousy. I knew he couldn't have gotten the same words from 9–9 because he didn't know how to ask the right questions, how to prime them for spilling their guts into the mic. Brown-nosing was his weapon of choice.

"That's because he didn't have a reason to say anything to you," I said more diplomatically before I took a sip of coffee. "He knew I had Mirage on tape ripping him to shreds."

"Well anyway," he replied, trying to suppress his obvious envy, "when you gotta have the piece in by?"

"I got about a week and a half but I want to get it in a few days early so I can show the white boys over there that black writers know how to get work in on time."

"I hear dat," he concurred before inhaling more salad. "Black-people time don't fly in white America. Just make sure you do a good job."

"I don't have a choice," I said. "I'm being honest with you when I say that this might be the most important thing I've ever written so far."

"Damn," he replied solemnly, as if a challenge was something to fear. "But what you doin' tonight? You goin' to that listening party tonight?"

Apparently the listening party, whichever one it was, was more important to him than my successfully completing the biggest piece of my career. Lamar had the attention span of a housefly. If the music industry ended tomorrow I could imagine him on his way to Hollywood in search of his next fix of glamour and glitz. He could tell you what and who was hot, who had sex with whom in the VIP room of the current club of the moment or who to call if you needed something from any record label in existence. But if you asked him to tell you the difference between two people's writing styles he'd freeze like a computer screen.

"Yeah I might go," I responded to his question. A ray of light pierced the gray sky above and splashed onto the sidewalk outside of the restaurant. I took it as a sign of some sort and looked at my watch. I had been sitting at the table for too long.

"Yo man, I gotta roll," I said while laying my half of the bill against the linen tablecloth. We slapped hands and I was on my way towards the exit.

"That piece is gonna kill 'em," he yelled like a fan to a star player just hitting the field.

Another splatter of bright daylight covered the gray brick-barriered park across the street. But the clouds quickly sucked it back into the heavens and I went south, down Madison Avenue towards 34th Street station, stopping at a newsstand for cigarettes. A few feet away a trumpet player piped solos for change. I plopped three quarters in his case and stopped to listen. Behind his dark aviator glasses I could see that one of his eyes was swollen shut. I stared at the injury as I lit my Newport, etching the image into my mind.

The man and his music stayed with me as I descended underground three blocks later. My inquiring mind wanted to know who had hit him and how he had ended up standing in that spot, undoubtedly hundreds of miles away from where he had played his first note. And he didn't stop playing, despite an injury that would have kept me at home and out of sight with an ice pack. That was dedication.

I wondered if I had that kind of discipline, if I could really do whatever it took to get where I wanted to be. Could I tell the story I was compiling, the one about two partners at a fork in the road walking away from each other? Would Delante Caution's plight ever make it to the shelf in my local bookstore? Did I have what it took to be the writer, the man, I wanted to be?

The questions rained down on me and something inside made me tremble for a moment. But then it stopped. I was overreacting. I'd been in the game since my sophomore year of college. Lamar was right. I was going to kill the world with that piece.

I ignored the blinking light on my answering machine and went straight to my desk and turned on my laptop. There was no time for phone messages. The hum of the disk drive told me that I was ready. The Windows insignia told me that I was set. I opened a new document and it was time to go. I now had everything I needed.

I played the 9–9 tape several times and put the new quotes in. Then I spent nearly four hours once again calling managers, label execs, and publicists. I was going to cover both men from every side and every angle. I even got a few words from the editor in chief at *Maintain*.

I was as thorough as I had to be. And as the clouded daylight turned into darkness I was still planted in my vinyl-cushioned fold-up chair, determined to finish it all in one night.

It was almost ten when I saved the new draft and threw premarinated strips of steak into a skillet, added broccoli, and put a fire under it. I boiled rice in a separate pot and dinner was on the way. I lit a cigarette, my first since Manhattan, and turned on the TV. There were a hundred channels and nothing was on. That was when the phone rang. I walked the length of the living room and I picked it up confidently, knowing that the cable and phone companies had already left their collection messages.

"Yo wassup Big D!" TD screamed into the phone. A thumping bassline and multiple voices played in the background.

"What's goin' on, partna?" I replied, trying to keep my sigh away from the phone's mouthpiece.

"You gotta come down here to this party at the Cooler. It's a lotta bitches down here. Plus I need to talk to you about somethin'."

I couldn't go out. I was sick of that life. What had going out to Joe's Pub or Speed or Carbon gotten me beyond too many drinks and too much wasted time? Here I was trying to create and someone wanted me to dive back into that cesspool of plastic stirrers and the same old faces. But something about his invitation had tickled my curiosity. And when TD wanted to talk he usually had something relatively important to get off his chest.

He was my best hip-hop informant in Harlem. From time to time he called me with story leads. In exchange I got him free CDs and passes into whatever shows and parties I didn't feel like going to. TD had dreams of rhyming, producing, and owning his own record label, the clichéd aspirations of every other knucklehead in the city. To hear him tell it he already earned high five figures a year working the streets in a handful of borderline scams and hustles. But despite my warnings no one could tell him that being a rapper wasn't exactly the way he had it in his head. The way he saw it, signing on the dotted line meant making it. Nothing could be further from the truth.

I'd met him at the Vibe Music Seminar, just after he'd finished up a year on Rikers Island for crack possession. He said he'd spent most of the bid reading a sizable chunk of the prison library, mostly business stuff, and claimed to have put a lot of his street earnings into bonds and mutual funds. In his master plan, those investments, coupled with his future rap earnings, would be enough to open up a chain of black-themed sports bars all the way down the East Coast. I was skeptical. On the rap end he hadn't gotten anyone besides me to even listen to his demo.

But aside from all of this he was at a party and he wanted me to be there. I didn't want or need to leave the house because I was trying to be a focused individual. But the first thing I learned on my way to manhood, in the back of a project courtyard, was that there are times when your friends need you. And you have to be there for them. If you are, they'll always be there for you. Besides, there might actually be some cuties in the house.

"Yeah I'll come through," I said as I stood up and stretched my back. "So what kind of thing is it?"

"It's like a launch party for some new magazine for black and Spanish women. And believe me they're all over the place down here."

"Well, in that case a young player like Mr. Grand might have to come down. I'll be out the door in ten."

"All right. I ain't goin' nowhere no time soon," he said before I hung up the receiver.

I scoffed dinner down like an animal. I took off my sweatshirt and changed into a burgundy button-up and decided to wear my blue Timberland coat. On my way out I stopped short as apprehension once again crept over me. I should have been doing something productive, going over the draft until I didn't have a doubt. But obsessing over an article wasn't my kind of night, at least not that night.

■   ■   ■

"WASSUP D?" RON, the Wednesday-night bouncer, asked politely as I stepped through the opened velvet rope and past the line in front of the venue. I didn't understand how bouncers could wear their T-shirts so tight. "Haven't seen you in a while."

"Not doin' that club column no more," I replied, stopping for a quick chat. "Magazine went out of business on me. Is it live in there or what?"

"Go and see for yourself," he said with a grin, before returning to the lengthening line before him. I gave him a nod and headed inside.

I'd met Ron in my first year in New York, back when he was working at a club called Groove and I had a contract with *Tango* magazine to cover black New York nightlife. In those first months I'd spent my nights in more clubs than I cared to count. But I did the best I could to remember the bouncers' names when they were given. Sometimes, if I was lucky, they remembered mine, or at least my face. Thus, when it came to downtown clubs, waiting in line was a once-in-a-blue-moon thing for me.

Upon entering, I scanned the shadowy faces beneath the room's deep blue lighting. Natural hairstyles and retro clothing met Fubu and Calvin Klein at every other square inch. It wouldn't be hard to find TD in a place that earthy.

I spotted him in no time. He was standing next to a metal post in slacks and a shiny silver shirt. A thick late-'80s-style gold rope hung from his neck and two empty glasses were in his large and veiny hands. He was zeroed in on the cleavage of the dreadlocked Jewish American princess standing in front of him, a thin metal ring through her nose. It took him a minute or two to see that I was standing right next to him.

"D! My man D!" he shouted as if I were on the other side of the room. He hugged me as if he hadn't seen me in years when it had only been months.

"I'm glad you came down," he said, grinning like Isaac from *The Love Boat*. "Ain't this party live man?" he asked.

As I'd expected, TD had done more than a little exaggerating. As I looked around there were only a few cute girls and all of them were stapled to the wall at the other end of the room, trying to be seen. The DJ was spinning trance, a music so monotonous that it was guaranteed to give the listener a migraine after the first ten minutes. Places like that gave me the impulse to find a seat at the bar and nod off. But there would be no rest for the weary.

"I guess it's all right up in here," I said, feigning excitement.

"I think I might finally have something," he said, lowering his voice and winking.

"What do you mean?"

"Well, I was talking to this dude in here a couple minutes ago and he said that he had his own label. So I rhymed a few verses for him and he gave me his card and told me he might want me to do a twelve-inch single for him." He grinned with each and every syllable, exposing his eight front teeth, all of which were shoddily encased in gold. He pulled the card from his shirt pocket and handed it to me. It read: "Shaka Muhummad, President and CEO, Hard Knock Records."

I'd never heard of the company. More important, any CEO who gave his card to someone for rhyming the way T did was more than a little suspect. I hadn't even seen the company name in any of those sixteenth-of-a-page ads that ran in the back of the second-rate hip-hop mags. Those two facts alone seated TD's potential deal into the shady section.

People like this Muhummad were usually bottom feeders, scavengers who made a living pimping guys like T into making them a nice grand or two if nothing else. Under their tutelage T's debut wouldn't even make it to the 99-cent bin at any major retailer. But then again, having heard T rhyme, I thought Hard Knock might have been the closest he would ever get to a real deal.

"So how's your girl?" he asked matter-of-factly before taking a sip from his Heineken.

"Who?" I asked, forgetting how long it had been since the last time we hung out. But he hadn't brought her up then.

"Your girl, your Xi . . . Xi . . . Xiomara?" I was surprised he got it all out. I usually cut people off before they could say it.

The time had flown faster than the Concorde, and the memories came back just as quickly. It had been almost a year since I had even seen her. She was the one who wouldn't fit into my space, the one that I had wounded all too willingly. TD had been one of the few there to catch the tail end when he saw us at Wetlands two nights before our unfortunate unraveling.

"Man I don't even mess with her like that no more," I said, laughing it off, a stinging pain building in my chest.

"Well, shit. Women! Here today, gone tomorrow, right? She was fine though." He gave me a sly grin before bursting into a drunken laugh.

"Yeah," I said quietly, "she was fine." To my right a quartet of industry regulars elbowed their way through the thickening crowd. I had seen them all before at different times and places. They were low-levels, the type who did everything for show out in public, buying expensive champagne with their phone-bill money and then adding ice that ruined the bubbly.

They pushed their way through the crowd like professional wrestlers on their way to a ring. The short, stubby one bumped TD as he passed, then turned around to give him a look of disgust. He should have let it go. I would have let it go.

"What the fuck is your problem yo?" TD yelled at them, his voice perfectly audible over the music. The DJ's trance was broken. All four of them stopped and about-faced like Imperial stormtroopers. Our rebellion was only two soldiers deep.

Short and Stubby gave us a face that said he was ready for whatever we had to give. But the others looked like deer in headlights. I had no business getting into a fight. The time for that had passed long before I'd even set foot in the Apple. I was grown. Grown men were supposed to talk things out.

But TD was my boy and boys backed each other up. It would've been stupid to lose a friend by going out like a chump. I cut through the crowd and snuck behind the opposing troops. If something did get started I wanted to catch my targets by surprise.

Words were exchanged, the kind of useless trash talk that isn't worth repeating. And it went on far longer than it should have, longer than it ever would have between two people who really wanted to fight. I should have tried to break it up, gone home to look over my piece one more time. But as I took my position, studying my targets for points of attack, I was thinking about the woman I'd wounded. The impending fight would be good for getting her out of my head.

Finally, TD was ready, as were his opponents. Short and Stubby had pointy ears and a beard that was trimmed into a single line that ran from one ear to the other. TD jabbed him in the face four or five times. Short and Stubby returned fire with a few blows. Two of his weak homeboys scurried out of the way while the third dug into his pocket for something.

If I was in Atlanta this would have been the part where I could have counted on my boy BJ to pull me out of the way so that he could take my place and fight for me. Or my boy Monty might have been around to for-tify my attack by landing a punch right before mine. But up in the Apple I was alone and vulnerable to everything that they'd tried to protect me from back then. I ad-vanced and hit my target with a left hook. He dropped like a sack of flour, his hand still in his pocket. An exhil-arating rush went through me.

But when I looked to my left I saw that the tide had turned against TD. He stumbled backward, a hair away from losing his balance. I moved in to give him a hand but before I got there something crashed against me and

I flattened against the linoleum floor. Moments passed and my body didn't move. More moments followed and I was still face flat, my nose pressed to the freshly waxed floor. A pair of arms lifted me to my feet. My back throbbed with pain.

"You all right?" Ron asked with professional concern. The other bouncer, Khalil, held TD in a tight full nelson.

"He's with me," I said as my legs found the strength to stand on their own. Khalil let him go.

"Both of you gotta break outta here," Khalil said more politely than I would have expected. I nodded in the affirmative as I scanned the room, still disoriented. Our foes were nowhere to be found.

"You okay?" TD asked as Khalil and Ron headed back toward the front door. "That stool musta hurt like a muthafucka."

"That's what they hit me with?" I asked. I winced in pain as I noticed the two prominent and darkening bruises on the right side of his face.

"Let's roll," I murmured. I didn't even get a chance to have a drink. Hennessy might have actually made the place bearable. But at least I'd kept my coat on. T hadn't, and had to go to the coat check while I waited for him by the exit.

Outside freezing rain came down in sheets. TD apologized for the whole thing and I told him not to worry about it even though I was in a new area code of agony. It had all happened so fast that I was more than willing to chalk the whole thing up to experience, as long as nothing else bad happened between there and my front door.

"Fights happen," Pop had told me during his last stint at our house. "Even when you're too old and too smart to be in them." It was one of the only decent pieces of advice he'd ever offered me. But my pain didn't totally have to do with mortal combat. I wondered where Xiomara was.

TD and I split up at the corner of 14th and Eleventh Avenue. I stopped and watched him seep into the mist before heading towards the 2 train in the opposite direction. A black-and-white feline rushed past me at the station entrance. I chose not to take it as bad luck and descended underground.

"This shit is gonna come back to you, Dakota," my last love had yelled at me as she charged out of my first studio uptown, a minute and a half behind the other girl, whose name I still couldn't remember. I couldn't really chase after her with my pants around my ankles. Months after that I'd crossed paths with her friend Kristin, who begrudgingly told me that Xiomara was in Japan working on some kind of documentary. I was happy because she'd always wanted to do movies. But that was all I knew. And the better part of me understood that that was for the best. As my back burned with blinding pain, I wondered if she'd just gotten her revenge.

The station was empty on the other side of the turnstile, the discouraging sign of a recently departed train. I couldn't stand still for long. So I paced the platform like it was my cell. My mind skimmed the highlights of my first would-be love gone awry. What had made me do it? What had made me set fire to the home we'd built when I had nowhere else to go? There had to be some logical reason. But after too much time I still hadn't found it.

A No. 2 train derailed my thoughts as it stopped before me with a late-night screech. I immediately noticed that there was a sleeping derelict in each of the front three cars. So I boarded the fourth, which was devoid of unsettling omens, and sat down. I positioned myself so that my back didn't press against the hard plastic seat behind me.

No one entered the car at any of the first five stops. It was so unusual that I checked my watch to make sure that time was moving, that I wasn't stuck in a lost episode of *The Twilight Zone.* I closed my eyes and waited for the muddled loudspeaker to announce Atlantic Avenue station. Behind my eyelids I imagined a psychedelic beach where the sand castles were green, the ocean waves purple, and the sound of the chiming subway doors echoing along with the waves. Then a pair of high heels clicked to a stop just in front of me.

"I didn't think I'd see you again," a familiar voice said. My lids opened like shutters to see her standing there, just as beautiful as I had remembered her. Maybe I *was* in *The Twilight Zone.*

"Carolina?"

"So you remembered my name?" she asked, grinning. "Why are you sitting like that?"

"I got in a fight," I replied groggily. "Hurt my back."

"You should have kept your hands to yourself," she said, grinning to herself even though the pain was far from funny. She eyed the empty row of seats directly across from me and sat down.

"What?"

"People usually don't get hit for minding their own business. Are you all right?"

"Yeah," I said as I sat up. "I'll be okay." Her presence seemed to take the pain away.

"You remember my name?" I asked, hoping that I had been as memorable as she was to me.

"No," she replied as she sat down on the bench across from me. "But I was going to ask you, if that makes you feel better."

"D," I said.

"Like the letter?"

"Yeah, the one that comes after C. So where do you live?"

"Crown Heights," she said. "I told you that the last time."

"Well that's not that far from me," I said excitedly. "I live in Clinton Hill."

"You told me that the last time too. So I guess you pay

too much rent to live with all the little trendy people over there."

"Well, maybe so, but I'm not your typical resident."

"I would believe that," she said.

"I'm glad I saw you again," I said.

"Why's that?"

" 'Cause I didn't want you to be the one that got away."

"I didn't know you were chasing me. But I guess I did get away from you the last time."

"Well, I don't want that to happen twice," I said with an honesty even I was surprised by. "Look, let's stop playing games. Let me just take you out to dinner or somethin'. I mean I just wanna talk, get to know you or whatever."

"Get to know me? Is that all you want to do?"

"I can't do anything else until I get that far, now can I?"

She smiled and produced a pen and a business card to scribble her number on the back of.

"Don't call me at work," she said, her eyes on her writing.

"I won't," I replied obediently. The train braked at Atlantic Avenue just as the card passed from her palm to mine.

"This ain't no fake number, is it?"

She shook her head with a slight grin. "I would have just said no again."

"Well I'll call you," I said, just before I jumped through the doors as they began to close.

I stopped and stood on the platform until the train was out of sight and then started out of the station towards my house. Though the pain from my injuries was returning, Xiomara had become a distant thought. I gripped Carolina's card tightly in my right hand, like I was a sixth-grader with my first phone number. I'd never asked a girl if her number was real before. But with Carolina Martinez I couldn't be sure.

When I got home I wanted to call her. It was 2 a.m. and I wanted to see if she'd answer. From what I knew she seemed like the kind of girl I could talk to until the sun came up, the kind you wore your best gear to go see, the kind who made you question what you were doing with your life. But I wasn't going to fold. I had a three-day waiting period. And I had to keep it in place.

■ ■ ■

"WE JUST WENT into the studio and did our thing," Fred B. said into my phone's receiver. I was finishing up a quick $500 profile for Lamar. His writer had backed out on him at the last minute and I was throwing him a much-needed rope. "This is the best album of our career. We're doin' this Bedrock style, baby!"

And it had been a long career for Fred B. and Wilma G., a husband-and-wife duo who had once hoped to be the Ashford and Simpson of hip-hop. They had a son and a daughter who were legally named Bam Bam and Pebbles. Personally I'd always thought that the whole Flintstones motif would have gotten them sued. But their lack of record sales must have saved them from that.

As a rap artist whenever you had something new you had to say it was the best thing you'd ever done to keep your hype going. And despite their constant coverage in *Maintain* (the editor in chief was friends with their publicist) their hype was running on empty.

"You're the first hip-hop duo that are actually a real married couple. How long have you been together and how do you separate the music from your relationship?" In the background I heard someone ask for a light.

"See, me and Fred, we keep it real," Wilma replied in her breathy, raspy voice. "My Boo and I been together for six years so this game can't tear us apart. And as long as the fans wants us out there we gonna find a way 'cause nobody else can do it the way we can."

In the tradition of canned answering I'd heard all of these statements before, so much so that my pen seemed to take notes on its own while my mind was elsewhere.

"Well, thanks a lot for the time," I said, happy to bring the thing to a close. "I'll make sure you get a copy of the piece."

"I-ight," Fred said before abruptly hanging up. I put the receiver in its cradle only to have it ring as soon as I'd dropped it.

"Hello?"

"Is this Dakota?"

"Yeah, who's speaking?"

"Hi, this is Mike Murphy from W. L. Pressman Press. Todd Markewitz gave me a copy of your novel, *Caution*. He said he talked to you a few days ago."

"Yeah," I said, feeling good that the man had decided to call himself. "He told me that you were going to read it."

"And I'm very happy that he did," he replied in a *Father Knows Best* kind of voice. "Needless to say we're very interested in publishing it."

"Really?" I said, keeping the tone of my voice as even as possible.

"Yeah, it's really different. I've seen stories like this before but you've done it in a very different, original way."

"Thank you," I replied proudly.

"But I've made some notes on your manuscript that I want you to look at, some edits and changes that I want you to make."

"And then you make me an offer?"

"Well it's never that easy, Dakota. I don't make the decision by myself. It has to go through our acquisitions board. But I think they'll see things the same way I do."

I paused, frozen with both excitement and nervousness.

"Wow . . . I mean that's great."

"But that's not what I want you to think about right now. What I want you to do is take a look at my notes and edits, give me a call and let me know what you think. And we'll go from there."

"Yeah . . . I mean yes, that's fine."

"If everything works out this is going to be Todd's first book as an editor. He found you so it's his project."

"That's great," I said. "I guess I'll be in touch."

"Talk to you soon," he replied before hanging up.

Edits and changes weren't going to be a problem. But instead of being excited I felt nervous. There had to be something else to it, some catch I wasn't paying attention to. But I couldn't think of anything. I didn't have time to think of anything. Because the phone rang again.

"Yeah?"

"D. How you doin'? It's Scott."

Scott Aldridge had a résumé that was pretty impressive. At twenty-four, he'd been a staff writer for the *Times*. At twenty-eight he was a senior writer for *Newsweek* and now at thirty-two he was out on his own, writing big features every month from his townhouse out in Plainfield. But more important, he was the best friend and mentor that I rarely ever saw.

"Damn! Yeah, I'm good man. Got a lot of good things goin' on."

"Nobody's giving you any drama, are they?" he asked. I was trying to save the good news for last.

"Well I saw your boy Allen Reeves the other day. The man tried to snub me a little bit on the street."

"Now you know Reeves ain't my boy. What did he say?"

"Man I bumped into him on a corner on the East Side. The thing was *he* tapped *me* on the shoulder. And then when I started tellin' him about what I was workin' on, he cut me off askin' me what I was readin'. And I started to tell him but he cut me off, talkin' about how I couldn't write if I hadn't read enough."

"Well . . ." he said with an elongated pause. "What *was* the last book you read?" he asked calmly.

"I finished *Black Boy*—"

"That was six months ago, D."

"No it wasn't!"

"I should know. I bought it for you for your birthday, punk." He had me and I knew it. "He's right, man. You can't write the word if you don't know the language, dude. And D, you're good. I told you that from the minute I read your stuff. But to do the art you have to understand the art. Look at me. How can I write about business and commerce if all I know is Redman and DMX? Or what if I don't do good research? I'd end up with sloppy pieces. You gotta take the time to get your reading done."

"He was just a asshole about it," I said. The fire inside was smothered into ashes.

"What are you gonna do, jump him at his office because he's an asshole? I'm going to give you some advice. Most of the people you meet in the game you're not going to like. You just do your thing until you find something else you can *and* want to do."

I'd met Scott at a workshop at City College on How to Stay Published in Print. After three hours of listening and taking notes I came up to him during one of the group exercises and gave him my clips. He told me that if he read mine he'd have to read everybody's in the class. I told him that I didn't care as long as he read mine first. And he did. He called me a week later and invited me to lunch.

Mostly we talked about writing, where I was from and where I wanted to be. He said he never had a desire to write fiction but he respected my dream and wished me the best. Since then we'd kept in touch. He checked in on me whenever he wasn't up to his eyeballs in work or out on business trips. I'd even come up to his place to house-sit on long weekends when he and his family went on trips.

"By the way," I said, trying to be nonchalant about it. "They might be publishin' my book."

"Who's gonna publish your book?" he asked enthusi-
astically.

"W. L. Pressman. They just called me right before you
did."

"W. L. Pressman? How the hell did that happen?"

"Some dude named Todd found it in the slush pile and
now they're talking about giving me a deal."

"When do you find out?"

"Well they're sending me some edits and changes
they want me to make."

"Oh, then you've got a while then. It can be a long
road to a check in books sometimes. It's a little harder to
get it right than an article."

"Yeah, I know. But at least it looks like I'm a little
closer to livin' your life."

He laughed.

"You know my life isn't that different from yours, D."

"You must be outta your mind. You doin' pieces on
wine and people in politics, record label presidents—"

"Yeah, but being the only black person in some of
those rooms ain't exactly a walk in the park. See, you
don't know about that part. You don't know about getting a call at your house from an editor who wants to
know how you feel about the Amadou Diallo shooting
because he doesn't know anybody else black to ask for
an opinion. You don't know about these little Ivy League
white boys fine-tooth-combing everything you do so

that they can find an excuse not to publish it. Man, I go through the same shit you do. Just on a different level. It ain't never easy for black people nowhere in this business, no matter how high up you are, especially when you're not trying to sell out. Plus my wife is always ready to kick my ass for never being home, hardly ever seeing my little ones."

I hadn't thought of it that way. From a distance all I saw were the big bylines he got and the checks that came with them. It looked like Easy Street. But the tone of his voice said that it never stopped, that once you got to the top of one mountain there was always another one to start climbing.

"I feel you on that," I replied, not knowing of anything else to say. "So what else you got goin' on?"

"Nothing really, man—" A crying child's voice suddenly entered the background and Scott responded. "Uh, look D, I got some *family* business to take care of. Then I gotta—"

"Look man, just handle yours," I interjected, knowing that my usual eight to ten minutes were up. "I'll holler at you soon."

"All right D. Take care."

Every time I got off the phone with Scott I had this sense of hope, a stronger belief that my dreams of a better career would come true. But I was a long way from where he was. I had to climb out of hell before I could get to his heaven. The Arbor Day article was a Goliath I had to topple. But I somehow felt like I was still searching for my stones.

■　■　■

MOST OF THE time I could have cared less when I dialed a new girl's number. The first few minutes were practically like a script. I tried to be as cute as possible, unleashing all kinds of stupid jokes and canned romantic comments. Sometimes they ate it up and sometimes they saw right through me. But I didn't want to do anything like that with Carolina. I just wanted to say what was on my mind. I had done it once already though, and ruined it all.

I'd barely been in New York a month when I met Xiomara at the Brooklyn Mod restaurant on DeKalb Avenue. It was a Friday and $15 of my first *Maintain* research paycheck had gone to two straight shots of Parrot Bay. Both had gone down like water.

The red lights above made her blue slacks and matching sweater look purple. A sliver of her navel was visible whenever she lifted her arms. And she was there alone, her pretty brown self sitting right next to me. But I was too scared to talk to her. Luckily, she asked me for the time.

"I don't have a watch," I said, the smooth buzz numbing my nerves.

"I'm supposed to meet my girlfriend here," she said. Her light brown eyes glowed in the colored light as her thick lips curled into a smile.

"She late?" I asked. Bob Marley's *Exodus* was being played track by track through the speakers.

"She's always late." She paused and looked at me.

"You're not from Brooklyn, are you?" she asked inquisitively. It wasn't hard to notice my drawl. I shook my head, feeling too shy and awkward to do anything else.

"Where are you from then?"

"Are you trying to pick me up?" I asked. The words had just come into my mind. She laughed, making me glad they had shown up there. I was also glad I'd come all the way from Harlem to check the place out.

"No, I'm from the ATL," I said.

"Where?" she asked confusedly.

"Atlanta."

"Oh, my aunt moved down there," she said, leaning in so she could hear me more easily over the music.

"A lot of y'all New York folks been doin' that."

"You got a problem wit' us?" she asked, smiling.

"If I did, I wouldn'ta moved here," I said.

It was an innocent beginning. But I wasn't innocent at the end. I kissed her in the cold air outside of Lafayette Avenue station, as I prepared myself for the long ride back uptown. She made me feel safe in a new city that seemed like it was always attacking me. But I didn't feel safe forever. I got scared, and fear had brought out the absolute worst in me, and invited it to stay.

I stuck to my guns and called Carolina on the third day after our *Twilight Zone* meeting. There was a tightness in my throat as the first ring came and went. She answered on the second.

"Hello?" she asked in a nonchalant tone.

"Yeah, Carolina, it's D. We met on the—"

"I remember, D. How's your back feeling?"

"It still hurts a little bit," I replied. "But I called to see how you're doin'."

"I'm good, thank you for asking. You're lucky you got me on the phone. I'm usually working late but I came home early tonight."

"Long hours in the computer business, huh?" I asked.

"When you don't have any help they get very long. What is it that you do again?"

"I'm a hip-hop writer," I said.

"So you write rap music?"

"No, I write about it. I guess I'm kind of like a journalist. You know, I review records and concerts, do interviews."

"It sounds interesting, going backstage and things like that."

"It's okay," I said.

"Just okay?"

"Lately it seems like it's all been the same. Hopefully I'll be doing something different soon."

"To be honest I've never liked rap that much anyway," she said bluntly. I smiled to myself. It was good to know that it'd take more than a pair of LL Cool J tickets to appease her.

But the conversation went on. She told me about Cuba and how she moved to the Dominican Republic after high school. There she got a citizenship hookup from relatives in high places and came to the U.S. as a Dominican.

I told her about Atlanta and how hot it got in the summers. We talked about how hard it was for both of us to adjust to all the snow and freezing temperatures. We talked about how hard it was to make friends, since neither of us had many of them, and we had a long discourse about why black and Spanish people ate so much pork. I told her all about my mother. Then we set a date at the Lemon in the Village on Friday night at nine. I went to sleep smiling.

I didn't know what to wear to the Lemon. Carolina had called earlier in the day to say that she was running late and wanted to meet me at the restaurant to save time. I ransacked my closet looking for something that wouldn't make me look like I was trying too hard to make a good impression. But at the same time I wanted her to notice me the very minute she spotted me at the bar.

I had a silk button-up that was absolutely out of the question, too many Polo sweatshirts, and three Tommy Hilfiger sweaters that would look good with practically everything. I grabbed the red Tommy and ironed a pair of khakis to go with it and my dark brown Rockport loafers.

It was just after seven and I wanted to be in the city by eight-fifteen so that I could check in with Maya over at her apartment. We'd set three different lunches that she'd canceled on and I wanted to catch her while I was in her neck of the woods. I had more than enough time since she only lived a few blocks from the restaurant.

A pigeon strutted along the subway platform at Clinton-Washington station. Every few minutes it flew up for a few feet and then landed back on the platform, sadly realizing that its return to the skies was blocked by the several feet of metal and concrete above. I wondered how it had ended up underground in the first place. But you could get lost anywhere in New York.

It was 7:28 when the C train finally bulleted across the tracks in front of me. Twenty minutes later I was walking down West 4th Street to Maya's apartment, a small loft tucked between NYU and Soho. It was unusually warm for February, almost 49 degrees.

A cab almost hit me as it ran a red light, and for a flash of a moment I wished that I was back in Atlanta, where cars and buses actually stopped for you. I crossed the intersection and turned onto the tree-lined brick-streeted block where Maya paid $2,000 a month to live.

"You must really like this girl," Maya said cynically, a spoonful of shredded wheat between her jaws. Fridays were her "Take care of Maya" days and her attire suited the occasion. Instead of modeling the latest in overpriced clothing she had on only a weathered Vassar T-shirt and a pair of pink sweatpants. Undoubtedly one of her sugar daddies would be through later to truly "take care" of her.

"What you mean by that?" I asked in defense of her comment.

"I mean look at you. You got khakis on and you're taking this girl to the Lemon. We don't even eat at the Lemon. Most of your little tramps will be lucky if they see Sizzler."

"But Sizzler don't have that ten-dollar shrimp and steak special this week."

"This girl must know what she's worth," she said with a smile. "I like that."

"Can you stop wit' all the jokes?"

"At least admit that you like her." She slid another spoonful between her full lips.

"I don't go out with girls I don't like," I replied.

She ducked and covered her head.

"I think lightning is about to strike!" she said while giggling.

"Fuck you," I replied. "I'm the way I am because I can't be lettin' these girls run all over me."

"Nobody runs over you but *you*, my dear," she said before looking up at the neon clock on the wall. "Well, you better get moving. I don't want to make you late. And I have some getting ready to do myself. Vincent is coming over at ten." I knew it.

"You're so see-through," I said while shaking my head. "Which one is Vincent?"

"You don't know him," she replied evasively.

"Well *this* is a first."

"He's not in the industry," she replied. "He's . . . he's a teacher."

"A teacher? You must mean like a yoga teacher, a Kama Sutra teacher, acupuncture, photography . . ."

"No," she said to cut me off. "He teaches at Boys and Girls High School, in Bed-Stuy."

I couldn't believe my ears.

"What, he won the lottery, inherited some money or somethin'?"

"No," she replied. "He just made me laugh." She was blushing. "I met him on the train and he started talking to me. I tried to play my usual 'bitch' routine but I couldn't help it. He's really nice."

"I don't think I've ever heard you say that about a dude in the whole time I've known you."

"Like I told you before, sometimes you gotta change, you get tired of things leading nowhere." Once again she looked over at the neon clock just above her canopy bed. "But I have to get ready, my dear. I'll tell you all about it."

"All right," I replied, still in a bit of disbelief. I kissed her on the cheek and let myself out. The elevator was open, empty and waiting for me. I looked down at my watch and realized that I was running late. This was not the woman to be late for.

I rushed up Sixth Avenue towards 17th Street, hoping to beat the clock. It was 8:50 and I was less than halfway there. I'd underestimated the distance between the Lemon and Maya's by almost ten blocks. I tried to flag a cab but it wasn't happening for *me* on a Friday night in the Village.

I unzipped my jacket for ventilation as the blocks oozed by. I was going to be late. I knew that she was going to leave if I wasn't on time. Fifteen minutes had passed when I finally got there. She was at the bar waiting patiently, her eyes counting every second on her black-and-silver timepiece. I tried to hide the fact that I was out of breath.

"And you told me to be on time," she said as she nibbled on the plastic stirrer in her cranberry juice.

"Something came up," I said.

"Yeah, I saw you running up here when I drove past you in the cab."

"Damn. Why didn't you stop and pick me up?"

"I was trying to be on time."

She had on black pants, a loose dark blue shirt, and short boots. Her hair was pinned up and she wasn't wearing earrings or makeup, neither of which she ever needed anyway.

"Are you gonna give me a hard time about this all night?"

"No. It was cute. You ran for me."

"Is that a good thing?"

"I guess it is. I'm still here, aren't I?"

"Well I'm glad we both here now. You do everything you had to do at work?"

"I never do everything I have to do at work. We've got a little server for a big office, not enough DSL connections, and every system in that place needs memory upgrades. But the CEO doesn't want to spend the money to do it right. So they pay me, and only little me, to make it work. But I can't lie. Deep down I love it. I love owning my own business, especially when it's going as well as it is now."

The plot to her story thickened as we got comfortable in our chairs. I learned that she had started her business in the Dominican Republic with a 486 desktop computer and a stack of homemade business cards. But there wasn't much work in a country where most people didn't have computers. So she worked every job imaginable for a year to save up enough money and favors to emigrate to the Rotten Apple, where she now lived with her uncle rent-free.

Her first job was working as a temp in an office that had three people out with the flu. Then she spotted a major problem with the company's server after several e-mails she sent hadn't been received by her supervisors. Someone there saw what they had in Carolina. Two weeks later she was hired full-time and in six months she had her first reference and almost immediately went out on her own.

"There's nothing else in the world I want to do," she said with salad in her mouth. Our entrees were taking forever to get to us.

We talked about movies and the similarities and differences between blacks in America and Afro-Hispanics in the DR and Cuba. She said that most people told you that racism didn't exist there. But it lives and breathes as it does anywhere else in the world. The forms it took were different though, particularly when you were as dark-skinned as most of the family she came from.

"You always ask me about me," she said. "Why don't you tell me something about you."

"There ain't really a lot to say about me. I'm from Atlanta and I'm a writer. I live here and I'm really enjoying bein' out with you. That's all you need to know."

She gave a narrow smile with perfect teeth.

"I'm glad I saw you again," I said. The words were an understatement. But I felt they were all I should say on a first date.

"So am I," she replied. "I wouldn't have had anything else to do tonight." I frowned. "Just joking," she said. "Don't be so sensitive."

Coffee came and went and we walked all the way down Sixth Avenue back into the Village. She wanted to play pool but we couldn't find a place that didn't have a mob ahead of us. So we ended up escaping the cold in the NYU student center.

"So what was your last girlfriend like?" she asked as if it were any old question.

"She was cool," I said, hoping that she didn't want to know more. I wasn't sure if I could tell her more without opening a very ugly can of worms.

"If she was so cool then how come you aren't with her anymore?" She knew she was poking at a sore spot, trying to see if I would react.

"I just wasn't the right guy for her," I said somewhat solemnly.

"So what did you do to not be the right guy?"

She wasn't making it easy. I wanted to tell her. Then

she'd know the kind of man she was dealing with. Once she knew she wouldn't expect anything from me. And if she didn't expect anything from me I wouldn't have to worry about the past, or the present, or any future with the beautiful, intelligent, and extremely cool woman in front of me. But once she knew the truth she also could have just gotten up and left. And I didn't want that. I really didn't want that.

"I'll tell that story the next time we go out."

"Hmm," she replied. "Got some secrets?"

"Everybody has secrets," I said plainly, relieved that she didn't seem like she was going to push the envelope. The Xiomara story was not the one I'd tell to cap off an evening.

"Yeah, I know what you mean," she said. She took a sip of hot chocolate and changed the subject, not giving me the reassurance I had been hoping for. After a half hour there we hit the streets again and found ourselves in a used CD shop on West 4th.

"So what do you believe in?" she asked as she fingered through a rack of CDs.

"What kind of a question is that?" I asked as I examined a marked-down copy of Labelle's *Nightbirds*.

"Because I want to know what kind of a person you are."

"You know you speak perfect English for someone who's only been here a few years."

"Thank you. I did a lot of practicing. Now please answer my question."

"I believe in God. I believe in my writing and I definitely believe in standing up for my people."

"Interesting," she said as she palmed a stack of CDs four units thick.

"What's so interesting about it?" I asked curiously.

"I guess I figured you might have said something else."

"Like what?"

"I don't know, like love or honor. You're a writer. I figured you'd be more . . . poetic."

"Well I believe in those too," I said. "What do you believe in?"

"Honesty," she said plainly. "Nothing but honesty."

We bought fourteen CDs between us, more of a stretch on my budget than hers. I lit a cigarette at the corner and took a deep drag. She shook her head and frowned with disapproval.

"You know you just lost some points."

"Why's that?"

"I can't stand cigarettes. I guess you don't believe in good health, do you?" I flicked the burning Newport into oblivion.

"I just quit."

"Oh, don't worry. I won't mention it again," she said disapprovingly. "But that's gonna change if you're around long enough."

"If I'm around long enough?"

"Yeah, if you don't mess up. Men have a habit of messing things up." We started across the street.

"Oh, so we mess things up?"

"What did I just say?"

"You just got it backwards," I replied.

She let out a sigh. "Whatever you say, papi."

From there we hit a bar called Caliente's for a drink and took the 6 train to Brooklyn Bridge station, where we split a cab. It was too cold for the long walk. The big yellow taxi raced us across the Brooklyn Bridge at riveting speed.

"It's so much prettier than the other ones," she said as she laid her head on my shoulder.

"What is?"

"The Brooklyn Bridge. It's my favorite bridge in the city."

"You have a favorite bridge?"

"I know it sounds stupid but when I was a little girl I used to go to the library and read books about America and New York. All the ones I read had pictures of the Brooklyn Bridge. It's strange that now I see it almost every day."

"Yeah. It always feels funny when your dreams actually come true."

"Yes, it does," she replied as we shared the moment. Ten minutes later we pulled up to my building.

"Well I really—"

"So did I," she said, cutting me off. "I'd kiss you but you got tobacco breath. Bring some gum next time." My face hit the pavement.

"Yeah—I'll have to do that." I handed her my part of the cab fare and turned toward my building, my bag of CDs swinging left to right as I walked.

"Be safe," she said. I turned around to catch the kiss she blew. The cab sped off, anxious to drop her off and return to the safer island of Manhattan.

I would've thought I'd be upset that I'd sprung for dinner and she didn't want to come upstairs. But I wasn't. There hadn't been a single ounce of drama. She hadn't gone for the most expensive thing on the menu and then not touched it. Nor had she spent our time harping on the old boyfriend that made her not trust men anymore. We had had a good time. That was unusual. But I liked it.

I didn't sleep much that night. Instead I parked myself at the computer and went through my Arbor Day piece. I scanned the text for holes and contradictions, made sure I hadn't misquoted anything or attributed information to the wrong source. Sometime around 4 a.m., when the birds outside my window began their day, I realized that it truly was the best I had ever done, that people were going to *get it*. I finally closed my eyes around four, thinking for a flash about Carolina Martinez and the warmth that I hoped we would share on a soon-to-come night. Dreaming of that, it was easy to sleep like a baby.

Date number two took place a week later. And she hadn't forgotten.

"So why did it end?" she had asked me at the end of our game at the Chelsea Piers. I had rolled a strike, finishing out our game in the bowling alley.

"You don't want to know," I said as I pulled off my bowling shoes.

"You promised. You're going to break a promise to me this early?" She wore a little girl's pout on her dark chocolate face.

"Nah," I said. "You sure you really want to know?"

"Yes, D."

"I cheated on her," I said plainly. She scanned my face to see if I was joking. It didn't take her long to see that I wasn't.

"Okay," she said, then paused again. "And why did you do it?"

"I don't know. Maybe I felt like she was too close, like she wanted too much from me."

"What did you think she wanted?"

"I mean I was startin' to get a lot of work and I was out a lot. So we didn't get to see each other but one or two times a week. And she went to bed early so I never wanted to call and wake her up." I stopped and looked at Carolina. She wore the same analytical expression she had on half the time.

"You still didn't answer the question."

"What kind of answer do you want?"

"The real one," she said. "Like I told you. All I ask is for you to be honest."

"I got scared," I said. "I think I was so worried that I was gonna fuck it up that I thought it was better to do it consciously than to do it by mistake. So there was this girl around my way. She wasn't even that cute. But she was there. And she made me feel like I was still in control, like I didn't have this *thing* hangin' over my head."

"That's what the relationship was to you? A *thing* hanging over your head?" Her voice was clearer than it should have been with the sounds of strikes and spares in the background.

"I hadn't really felt that way before. I was used to feelin' like I could walk away at any time and no one would ever miss me. Always seemed to make things easier."

"Do you think you'd ever do that again?"

I felt like a little kid in detention, thinking of nothing but when I'd be dismissed. Would she dump me on the spot based upon my answer? She didn't seem like the type to want to get involved with that kind of drama.

"I don't know," I said. "I guess since then I sorta felt

like if someone came along that didn't make me feel like that when we got close I'd be fine. But I haven't been that close yet."

"Okay," she said. A short pause followed. "Let's go down to Jerry's and get something to eat. I'm starving." Shoes in hand, she darted towards the skate counter. I had been waiting for a speech, a paragraph, even a single sentence on how it made her feel. But there was nothing, the kind of nothing that kept you on eggshells, checking under your car before you started it every morning. The blast never came. But I was always on guard, hoping that I'd clipped the right wire on that very deadly device.

SPRING

HE WATER WAS a little too hot. But I liked it, especially the way it made her lips feel as they
moved up and down on me. I wrapped my arm around
her and pulled her close. We kissed time and time again
with the water cascading down our faces. Then she
stopped and stepped entirely out of the bathtub, dripping wet, and walked out of the bathroom. I followed. I
knew what came next.

There was something about our cold wetness that was
thrilling. Our nipples rose hard and thick as we playfully
slipped and slid against each other. She moaned loudly
as my tongue entered her, the sound bouncing off of the
echo-creating bedroom walls.

We knew how to work each other. The water and
sweat soaked into the mattress as we scrambled across its

surface. She climbed on top, tightening her walls, knowing what it did to me. Our orgasms collided, just before the alarm went off. We crashed to the mattress like lifeless dummies.

"We gotta start getting up earlier," she said, breathing heavily. She wiped herself off with the comforter and stood up at the foot of the bed. "I think I need two of these before I go to work. One just doesn't get me through the day anymore."

"If you worked from home like me you'd have all the time you need," I said, smiling and out of breath.

"But I can't fit a hundred computers into my room," she said as she passed the blanket back to me, damp. I grabbed the top sheet and pulled it off of the bed for my own wipedown.

"I've asked a million times already, but how come you make fifty thousand a year and live in a room in your uncle's house?"

"Because that's all I need," she said. "I send money to the DR for my parents and my little brother, pay my bills, do a little shopping, and help my uncle with his expenses."

"But he ain't broke. He owns a store."

"D, how many times do I have to tell you this?"

"Tell me what?"

"That I live my life the way I want to. Just be glad I'm keeping you in it."

"Well excuse me. But I'm sure your mornings wouldn't be as exciting without me."

"Hmmm. I guess you're right about that," she said with a grin before moving over and kissing me on the cheek.

"But I gotta run, baby." She jumped back up and climbed into the navy-blue business suit that was her favorite. Now all she needed were her shoes and jewelry, which she retrieved from the bathroom in record time.

"You know what today is?" I yelled into the bathroom.

"Yes I do, D."

"You gonna read it?"

"Yes I'm going to read it, D." With heels, earrings, and the twin silver bracelets she always wore, she was ready for her commute into downtown Brooklyn.

"You gonna miss me?" I asked.

"I always do," she said just before she kissed me on the cheek again and rushed towards the door. "But I'm five minutes late. I'm out—"

The door slammed shut behind her. I'd gotten used to her quick exits.

Winter had shifted to spring and everything was great. *Caution* was set to be published the following winter and I was even starting to get work from the *real* magazines. And the people over at *The Magazine* and places like *Gear* and *Maxim* were pretty good about getting me my checks on time. I was happy, and Carolina was the jewel in my crown.

It was the Day, the one I had been waiting for for nearly three months as my story on the artists formerly known as Arbor Day would finally reach a circulation of more than three million people. It had been a lifetime of edits and visits to the magazine office with Chad. He'd cut some of my best phrases, but it came with the territory. As long as I was getting a byline in his magazine, losing a few words here and there didn't matter.

A half hour later I was checking the weather on my new TV with my new and very illegal cable descrambler box. Two hundred channels for what I paid for basic cable. My book advance had made all the movie channels and pay-per-view absolutely free. The high was going to be 65 so I took my sky-blue Polo sweatshirt and a pair of matching jeans and laid them across the sofa.

The magazine had hit stands at 6 a.m., and though I could have gotten copies days before, I wanted to wait until it was in the hands of the people. I wanted to ride the train and see readers' eyes glued to the article. That kind of attention meant far more than the $5,000 paycheck I'd gotten for it.

The Day was going to be spent running around. I had to get my courtesy copies from *The Magazine*, run by Todd's office to drop off the first galleys of my novel to the production editor, and then go by *Maintain* to give Lamar a loan for a plane ticket he needed. He was flying to the "How Can I Be Down" convention in London and *Maintain* was too cheap to pay for him to go. And to round the day out I was supposed to have dinner with Carolina at the Joloff Restaurant back in the neighborhood since she was working late for the rest of the week and I probably wouldn't see her.

I flipped through the freshly delivered *Daily News* looking for positive current events but gave up just before I got to the sports section. I switched Thundarr the Barbarian on my 34-inch screen and listened to the bell in the church down the street. It signaled 10 a.m. I had to get moving.

On the train a bearded and wrinkled Jewish man shotgunned leaflets to apathetic commuters on his way through my car and towards the next. I took his offering and ran my eyes over the tiny faded print trying to find what it was that he was selling. Even if it didn't cost I knew he was selling something. I looked down to see that his urgent message was a stack of stapled pages, Biblical prophecies that had supposedly come true during the second half of the twentieth century. The last page even contained prophecies specifically for the African-American community. I thought about reading it but folded it up and stuffed it in my bag, dooming the information to be lost forever.

The Magazine was on the twenty-sixth floor of a sky-scraper near Rockefeller Center. It wasn't my usual part of town and I still got the building confused with the Fox News building further down Sixth Avenue. But the absence of Fox's midday lunch traffic near the entrance let me know that I was at the right place.

Upstairs, the lily-white receptionist once again mistook me for a messenger and pointed me towards the courier drop-off window. I told her I was there to see Chad and she motioned me to go in without a word. I made a left towards the editorial department, where they were already waiting for me.

"There he is, the man of the hour," Chad yelled across the entire section with the voice of a game show host. "This month's special cover man, Mr. Dakota Grand!"

Scattered applause rang throughout the office. Some people even stood up. There, on the edge of the room, it was good to be able to see the occasional dark face among the many white ones. But I still felt like the butt of a joke I didn't understand.

"What's goin' on?" I asked Chad as we shook hands stiffly.

"You're what's going on," he said with a sly grin. "Everybody around here is in love with your piece. Who knows? It might turn out to be some award-winning shit."

"Well I won't hold my breath on that one," I replied with a flash of teeth.

"No man, I'm serious. Rap artists maybe make a cover once a year but everyone agreed that your piece belonged there. Looks like you're in there, man."

"Well thanks," I replied, on the verge of blushing. But I wanted to make sure that I wasn't going to be a one-hit wonder. "I hope I can do somethin' else for y'all," I said humbly.

"Oh, you don't have to worry about that," he said as if he were speaking to a child. "We're already figuring out what to give you next."

Various members of the magazine staff approached and welcomed me like deacons do baptismal candidates. We shared words about lunch dates, meetings, and working on a contract basis. I had arrived. And I was ready to milk it for all that it was worth.

"So how did you start writing?" Claire asked before taking a sip from her Heineken an hour later. The editor in chief had invited me out to lunch at the Skylight Diner on Eighth Avenue. She looked like she was in her mid-thirties, a cross between Sharon Stone and Kathleen Turner. Her long blond hair was ponytailed behind her. Flanked by Chad on the left and Dan, the half Puerto Rican, half Asian managing editor, on the right, I felt like the final piece in a multiracial puzzle.

Claire told me that she had gotten her start in Atlanta as well, working as an assistant editor at *Atlanta Magazine*. It wasn't a hotbed for minority news and views but I had always liked the writing. Nevertheless it felt good to know that she knew a little about where I came from. Chad nodded along with her words like a TV reporter being filmed for reaction shots.

As they talked I looked around at the diner. The place had a '50s diner feel to it: neon signs in the windows, the old-school stools along the lunch counter, curving booths with circular tables in the middle. But we were '90s journalists personified: fresh haircuts, record-label T-shirts, jeans and khakis. Dan's cell phone came alive and he squirmed out of the booth towards the foyer to take the call. Lamar would have just yapped into the mouthpiece right in front of us.

"It's both a long and short story, Claire," I replied after a sip of water. "I wrote my first short story when I was nine. It was a class exercise but I really got into it. So I wrote more stories and then some poems. And it just grew like a plant. I published my first article in a local paper when I was twelve. The next thing I know I'm sitting here at a table with you."

"Twelve, huh? What was I doing at twelve?"

"I wasn't thinking about writing. I know that," Chad said.

"You definitely have it together," she replied. Dan casually returned to the table.

"I just can't wait to get back to work," I said after a brief period of silence. Once again I was met with nothing but smiles.

"Just scored a cover and he's already on to the next thing," Dan chimed in, as if he had been there all along. "It's good to see that you're hungry."

"That's the only way to be," I replied. Dan gave me a nod and grin of approval.

"Our editorial meeting is tomorrow so Chad will give you a call in the morning. We'll definitely have something else for you."

"But you gotta promise me something," Claire said with a warm smile.

"What?" I asked.

"Take today and enjoy your cover. Worry about your next piece tomorrow."

"I'll try," I said. "But I'm always thinkin' about tomorrow."

I shook each of their hands before departing, happy to put a line through another appointment on my schedule. I was also glad to be on my way to an office that had more color. On the street I lit a cigarette and fantasized about what assignment they would give me next. What would it take to move up in the ranks, to have them panting for the next big thing with my name on it?

I made a quick run into W. L. Pressman at 43rd and Sixth to leave the galleys for the production editor with the receptionist. I'd told Lamar I'd be there at three and I still had five minutes to be on time. Luckily *Maintain* was only a few blocks down Fashion Avenue. I knew that Lamar needed his money as soon as possible so I hopped into a cab just letting someone out and was on my way down to his building.

"Deez streets is madness," the Rastafarian cab driver yelled over the blaring boom of Burning Spear. I'd never ridden with a driver with such a loud system. I didn't think that cabbies were even supposed to play music at all. "You never know who you gonna bump into and what they want. You remember dat, ya-ear?"

"I hear you," I said, wondering if he was somehow talking about my life. The bass-driven rhythm gave his words a strange importance. It also made the cab rattle. He cut a sharp left on 39th and then made a right on Lexington and we were there before I realized it.

"Wake up boy," the Rastaman yelled playfully as I snapped out of it. The cab was double-parked in front of the *Maintain* building. I handed him five singles.

"Wassup, D?" Fernando asked as I bypassed the visitors list and headed straight for the elevator. Fernando was the head of building security, a bulky Puerto Rican who had dreams of pro boxing when he wasn't keeping the building out of danger. I took him to lunch once back when I worked up in research because he'd spotted a FedEx guy about to deliver one of my packages to the wrong floor. Since then we were always cool and cordial.

Something touched me when I pushed the button for the elevator. It was cold and fluttery, a feeling and a voice that told me to turn away and go home. It told me that Lamar could get the money later. I toyed with complying and then I fully decided to do so. I would just run the dough by his apartment later, or come by when he was leaving at seven. But before I could turn towards the exit the center elevator's doors opened. It was too late.

Mirage stood three feet in front of me like Darth Vader 2000, two medium-sized soldiers beside and behind him. I noticed a copy of *The Magazine* held tightly in his fist.

"You!" he yelled as if I'd just murdered his best friend.

"Hey Mirage, what's goin' on?" I was too high on the day's events to see that his bloodshot eyes spelled anger all around.

He took two steps forward and answered with a fist that knocked me flat on the floor before I figured out what it was. I tried to get to my feet but his boys were already on me. As if on cue they grabbed both of my arms, pulled me to my feet, and held me there.

"What the fuck is this shit you wrote about me?" he asked before practically ramming his fist through my abdomen. I wanted to double over but they held me upright. I hoped that Fernando was dialing for help, or arming himself with some kind of a weapon. But he'd probably just ducked down. There was no prize for him to win in that fight.

Mirage followed up with an uppercut. And after that the pain flooded in from everywhere. I had to do something. Rule number one back at home on Fair Street was that if you got jumped you had to at least get one good shot in before you went down. They had my arms but my left leg was in perfect alignment with his groin.

Mirage was doubled over on the ground in seconds. I shook one arm loose and hit the one to my right with the dreads and matching beard. That was when my highlight reel ended.

Fists and heels rained down in buckets. A bone snapped and pain flooded through my right arm. I heard other voices and took more blows as I curled into the fetal position. I closed my eyes and tried to get my mind somewhere else but I didn't make it. I couldn't black out either. Was I dying? Was my clock being punched at the ripe old age of twenty-two? Then, ever so slowly, it began to stop. The voices faded to an echo and finally it all dissolved into darkness. I wasn't happy anymore. I was never going to be happy again.

■ ■ ■

I HAD A dream. I was sitting in a bar pouring rum onto a long gash on my right forearm. It was Brugal, Carolina's rum of choice, and it stung like a hive of wasps all poking at one spot. Mirage was behind the bar in a vest and white shirt looking like an oversized Isaac from *The Love Boat*. He looked at me with an empty expression and then began to speak.

"It ain't your fault but you better do something about that. You can't live with that."

"What should I do?" I asked.

"You better take care of that," he said. Then he walked down to the other end of the bar and started washing glasses as if it were the only thing left to do. I watched him wash for what seemed like forever before I opened my eyes into the sterile environment of a hospital room.

Lamar sat next to the bed in a chair with his head hung low and his hands clasped, looking more reverent than I had ever seen him.

"I'm alive," I said with uncertainty as I struggled to speak. He looked up at me with a melancholy expression.

"Yeah, you alive," he said solemnly, and then a pause. "But you ain't looked in the mirror yet."

I didn't need a mirror. Lamar's expression had said it all. I soon learned that Mr. Arbor Day had blessed me with a concussion, a broken arm, three fractured ribs, and a body full of cuts and bruises. The doctor said that it was a miracle that there was no internal bleeding.

"Did you call Carolina?" I asked as if it should have been a natural reflex.

"I ain't got her number," Lamar said, as if the idea had been out of the question.

"I gotta let her know I'm all right. We supposed to have dinner."

"Dinner? Man you ain't nowhere close to bein' all right. You definitely gonna need to reschedule."

"I gotta let her know what happened," I said frantically. "There's no way she could know what happened."

"I hate to tell you this. But there ain't too many people left that *don't* know what happened. After you got your ass beat down in the lobby, people up at the office went to the phones like somebody had shot the president. You should be just happy you ain't eatin' your food through a straw or somethin'."

"Tell me you ain't serious?" I asked, painfully realizing that I, Dakota Grand, had already become another piece of gossip for every set of ears in the industry. I was Tyrone Fields. I was WWII. I was just another victim.

"Since when do people keep their mouths shut? You just got your ass whipped by a major rap star!"

I closed my eyes and listened to the comfortable hum of the fluorescent lighting overhead. Somewhere in that darkness I found peace in the fact that at least I could sleep it all away. Fifteen minutes later I had Lamar call Carolina on her cell phone. She was sitting in my room before dusk and stayed there until dawn.

I stayed in that bed for three days, weaving in and out of sleep. My crew came in shifts. Lamar came by in the mornings, Maya in the afternoons, and Carolina brought up the rear after she got off of work. I hadn't expected for them to keep me there that long, so I was glad I'd invested in a good health care plan. But I needed to get back home to make full sense of what had happened, so that I could somehow try to repair the damage, make things right.

As far as the attack went, Lamar explained that I had just been a victim of bad timing and circumstance. Mirage's weed habit had had him scraping the sky at the time of our interview. So of course he hadn't remembered a single word he'd said. Therefore, when he read the article he was convinced that I was a liar, even though I had him on tape.

After that he was on a seek-and-destroy mission. So he'd gone up to *Maintain* to do an interview with Lamar, one that would supposedly set the record straight in the following month's edition. His primary target just happened to be getting on the same elevator he was exiting.

"Mr. Grand?" the well-dressed man asked from the hospital doorway. I was busy reading the new *Fluff* but set it down to see what he wanted.

"Yeah," I replied. "Who are you?"

"My name is Randall Brown and I'm one of the attorneys for Vertigo Records."

"Let me guess, Mirage's lawyer, right?"

"Did the suit give me away?"

"No jokes," I said, my expression stiffening. "What are you here for?"

"I heard about you being assaulted and I wanted to come down and see how you were."

Perhaps it was the moist S-curl, or more likely the expensive alligator shoes, that told me not to trust him. If I let him he would have massaged my ego for an hour before he got to the point.

"All right Randall. Look, I write about this stuff all the time—"

"And you write so well—" he began to chime in. If I wasn't in pain I would have laughed at his attempts at brown-nosing.

"So you guys are worried about me pressing charges. Puttin' your boy Mirage upstate?"

"We don't want you to do anything that isn't necessary."

"Necessary?"

"Sending my client to prison isn't going to get you out of this bed any faster. Besides we've got two men who will testify that Mirage didn't lay a finger on you." He raised two caramel fingers to accentuate the point.

I hated cops and judges. No matter what laws I lived under, I'd never seen myself taking part in putting another black man behind bars. I had too many childhood friends in those places. My father was in one. Besides, I knew that Randall's $2,000 shoes proved he wouldn't let his client get convicted.

I flashed back to Mirage's face, just before the first punch had been thrown. I thought about the first time I heard "On a Roll," at my boy Mikey's house the summer before we started the tenth grade. I remembered the way I played the single in my deck until the tape got warped. I remembered all the posters and paraphernalia I still owned. I had revered those two men like classic quarterbacks. And now one of them had put me in the hospital.

As a man, when you pressed charges, it was like getting someone else to do the dirty work. The whole world would have looked at me as less of a man for it. People who lived in the streets, my hip-hop readership, didn't handle their business that way. So I told myself that I shouldn't either.

I thought about all the men who'd been attacking us

journalists, the threats we'd found in our mailboxes. I thought about all the stories I'd written that protected rappers like Mirage, portraying them in a positive, productive light they'd never get on the evening news. And I'd gotten nothing but a concussion, bruises, and a broken arm for my efforts. I wasn't going to hide behind the cops, or *The Magazine*, or anyone else. Someone had to do something. And I was the only one with my hand raised.

"Thanks for the offer," I said. "But y'all ain't buyin' me off."

"Do you realize that if you do press charges you'll be waging a war not just with Mirage but with the billion-dollar corporation that owns him?"

I couldn't believe that the Ebony Man in front of me had actually gone as low as saying that they owned him, that he was their property. But that wasn't my concern.

"Oh don't worry," I replied. "I'm not pressing charges. But I'm not taking the money and I'm not signing a goddamn thing. All I want is for you to give Mirage a message for me."

"And what's that?" he asked coldly.

"Tell him that it ain't over."

"Is that all?" he asked.

"Yeah," I said. "You can leave now." He about-faced and exited like the soldier he was. I let out a sigh of relief.

I wasn't sure what I was going to do. I wasn't sure if I even wanted to take it beyond what I'd already set in motion. There was the risk of him coming for me, of me having to face him again, with only one arm to defend myself. But more than likely he would stay out of the way, let it all blow over, stay in the studio and keep making tracks for his next gold record. I'd taken my stand, and I just wanted to go home.

But traumatic experiences aren't that easy to let go of. And as I sat there in that bed for the rest of the day I thought about Mirage nonstop. His voice was in my ears, the impact of his first blow playing on a loop in my mind. They had broken my writing arm, the one I used to take notes, to type stories, the one I wrapped around Carolina when we walked down the street. I was sure that he knew all of that, that he had consciously chosen to cripple me as a reminder of what happened to those who told the truth, who refused to bend to his will. And while others had thrown in the towel I was not going to bow down. I had told the truth and he was going to admit it, to me, no matter what I had to do. Until then I was going home, to heal and to wait.

When I was finally discharged, Maya came to ride home with me, since Carolina had to work. On the elevator to the street it occurred to me that I hadn't called Mama to tell her what had happened. But after only a little thought I knew that that was the best. I didn't want her to worry. I didn't want to give her the ammunition for another firing squad lecture about my career choice and why I should come back home. I'd tell her after the fact. She was too far away to help anyway.

The skyscrapers giggled at me as we cabbed away from the hospital. The Brooklyn Bridge joined in with a gut-busting laugh as we rolled over it. I thought I heard something about me and Mirage on the radio just before we got out of the car. A chubby dark-skinned kid in an Arbor Day sweatshirt walked past my building as I approached the entrance walkway. Mirage was everywhere.

"You're taking this way too seriously," Maya had said in the cab, her arm around my shoulder. "There are nuts like that guy everywhere. He just happens to be a rapper whose music we all like."

"That's not the point," I replied with a military sternness as I looked down into my lap. My ribs ached sharply.

"I know," she said. "But my point is that I don't want you to overreact. You just need to forget about it. Get your girl to come over and take care of you and—"

"That's exactly what I don't want," I almost yelled. "Just because I'm hurt don't mean that I can't take care of myself. I got a lot of planning to do and I can't afford to have no innocent bystanders get in the way."

"Innocent bystanders?" she asked with a quick laugh.

"What are you, Batman now? Driver, can you turn around and take us to Bellevue. You need some time in the psycho ward, D. You might be going postal. Carolina's the one girl you *need* to be with," she added. "You can trust her."

"It's not about trust," I said, staring at the driver's blurry ID behind the Plexiglas. "She just can't understand what I'm about to get into."

"Neither can I," she replied, shaking her head. "You sure you don't want to head back uptown? They got a nice padded cell waiting for you."

"That's not funny," I said, even though a smile tried to force its way onto my face.

"No, it's not," she said very seriously. "I know you. And as someone who loves you I'm telling you that you need to get it together. You need to go home, put your feet up, and wait until it's time for that cast to come off. Trust me, everything will be the way it was in no time."

She really thought that that was true, that the injuries had only done bodily damage. Maybe it *was* smarter to just get over it. But for me it was about something deeper, about the disrespect of being nearly slaughtered in a building lobby, just because I told nothing but the honest-to-God truth. Something inside of me had been torn and I couldn't just stitch it back together. But I had to do something about it. And until I did, everything else had to go on hold.

Carolina called just before five to tell me that she was on her way over. I was lying in the bed, my cast across my chest, arm still in the sling.

"I'm stopping by the grocery store to get us some dinner," she said, her voice distorted by the cell phone.

"That's all right, babe. I think I just wanna be by myself tonight."

"But you just got home from the hospital, D. I want to make sure—"

"Look, I done got hurt before. I just don't need company right now. I'll call you later on."

There was a long pause, her good intentions crushed under the weight of my words.

"Well, okay. You sure, papi?"

"I'm sure, baby girl. I'll holler at you a little later on." I hung up the phone, not sure if I had done the right thing. But I couldn't afford the risk. I couldn't have anyone, even her, too close.

I spent the rest of the night and the following day trying to lay still on the couch, soaking my brain in movies and music video. The doctor had warned me that I had to be careful until my ribs fully healed. Too much movement could create a pocket of air between my ribs and lungs that could suffocate me to death. Pain shot up my right side whenever I reached for a glass from the

cabinet or for the juice in the fridge. I was low on groceries but I wasn't sure if I could make the full walk to
the bodega. But I definitely couldn't carry anything
back. So as I opened my last can of Pepsi, I sat back
down and assessed my situation, only to come to one
twisted conclusion: that Mirage had planned all of this.

He wanted me to suffer until I killed myself from the
pain and frustration. He would fly down to Atlanta on
the same plane with my corpse only to spit on my grave
after the funeral. He was probably across the street with
a telephoto lens watching me drag myself around the
living room struggling to open one of my cans of Camp-
bell's Chunky soup. There had to be a way to get him
back. I just had to find it.

But in the meantime life had to go on. New assignments floated in from several places and I got to work. I
wasn't going to let Mirage destroy my career too. I had
to balance my cast at just the right angle so that my fingers could reach the laptop keyboard. It was cumber-
some, but I typed when I needed to. I knocked each
article down like a bowling pin and then had a few shots
of my private stash of Hennessy to celebrate its completion.

I needed advice. But Scott was out of town covering a
voter registration drive in Florida. Maya was visiting her
sister in Cape Cod and Lamar was under pressure trying
to close his sections at *Maintain*. So I called the one

person I normally wouldn't have when I really needed someone to hear me: my mother.

It took a moment for me to remember the number. But I dialed and it rang. It rang again and then she picked up.

"Hello?" she responded in that bookkeeper tone she usually used at work.

"Ma, its me. How you doin'?"

"Well. Well. Well. Look who decided to call me."

"I know it's been a while, but I've been busy, Ma."

"Oh, I'm sure you have. I got that article you sent me. Looks like you're movin' up in the world up there. That's a magazine I've actually *seen* before." That was her version of a compliment.

"Thanks, Ma," I said, actually proud to receive her version of a compliment.

"How've you been otherwise? You still with that—"

"Nah, Ma. We broke up a long time ago. But look, I called you because I wanted to talk to you."

"I don't have any money if—"

"No, Ma, I don't need money. I haven't asked you for money for a long time. I got hurt, Ma. I was in the hospital. I just—"

"Oh my Lord," she said, the maternal warmth raising the pitch in her voice. "What happened?"

"Well you know that cover story I said I was doin'? Well the dude I wrote it on, he didn't like it and he and some other dudes beat me up, broke my arm and fractured some ribs." My voice almost cracked as I said the words. "I just got out of the hospital." There was a long pause. She was not the person to talk to about this. And I should have known it.

"You never listen to me do you," she began. "How many times have I told you you need to go back to school and get your degree, get a job at a real paper and some benefits? Then you won't be getting beat down in the street by all those hoodlums."

"God, Ma," I sighed, begging for some sympathy. "You seem to care more about your son getting a degree than him gettin' his arm broke." I could hear the incoming lecture on its way.

"I cared for you long enough to raise you didn't I? Then you had to go on off to New York and do what you wanted to do. Now you're sittin' in a hospital bed. I hope you're happy."

"I'm not in the hospital anymore. But see Ma, this is exactly why I don't call you. You don't never have nothin' supportive to say. Just because I didn't do what you wanted me to do, almost *three* years ago, you not gonna care about me now? It would make me feel better to know that's somewhere under there, that you care about me, that you care about your only son." I knew that she cared. It just never felt like it.

"I pray for you every day, son. But if you'd listened to me in the first place you wouldn't be hurtin' right now."

"I couldn't listen to you, Ma. I couldn't do it your way. I had to do what I had to do."

"Yes you did," she replied sarcastically. "So you had to go and live the *crazy* life, chasing around after all those thugs and drug dealers. *My* son knows that he can come home whenever he wants to. He knows that I'll do my best to try and help him do it right the second time."

"I'll see you at Thanksgiving, Ma," I said, admitting defeat. Thanksgiving was eight months away.

"I hope I hear from you before then," she replied earnestly.

"You will, Ma. I love you."

"I love you too," she said just before she hung up the phone.

Something left me when I turned that phone off. It might have been the last iota of hope that I could make her happy, that at some point I could be who she and Maya and Lamar and even Carolina wanted me to be. I knew that she had worked hard, a full-time job, seasonal work on some weekends. But I couldn't have her tell me who I was. She hadn't even listened enough to know what I was up against. I had to do this *my* way, on my own. The phone still tight in my hand, I rose to my feet.

I had to write something, something to celebrate my emancipation from trying to please other people. I was officially doing it for no one but myself. No Maya. No Lamar. No Carolina. I had missions that had to be accomplished and if anyone didn't like it they could walk. I would survive on my own.

I was going to walk over to the laptop and write something that said all of that, something I could re-member in case such times of hardship ever came upon me again. I moved my left foot forward and forgot that I was standing behind the coffee table. My shin slammed against the hard oak and I fell forward, tripping over the entire piece of furniture. As gravity pulled me violently toward the wood floor, my right side, the side with the fractured ribs, pointed downward. I stretched my right arm out to protect my cast from the impact. But my ribs were another story.

I screamed in agony as I smacked against the ground like a chunk of raw meat. The pain shot through the en-tire right half of my torso, exponentially worse than anything I'd felt reaching up to the cabinet. It was like lying on a bed of thick-needled cacti. I screamed again. I knew that I could get up, eventually. I just wasn't sure if I wanted to.

I had called my mother for love and comfort and had gotten nothing but another lecture. That wasn't what I wanted. What I wanted was someone who was going to tell me that I was going to make it back up, that it was going to be all right.

Slowly my good arm and legs got me upright. I bent down and picked up the phone, which had slid a few feet across the floor when I fell. I dialed a number, paged someone, and hoped that she'd call back. And of course, she did.

"Are you done with your little control-issue thing?" Carolina asked, the humming sound of CPUs in the background. I had the impression that she was smiling.

"I think so," I said. "Can you come see me tonight?"

"Of course I can," she said affectionately. "I'll come by when I get off work."

"See you then," I replied.

There was a knock on the door early the next morning, just after eight. I slowly made my way over to the keyhole to see two white men in their thirties looking directly into the fisheye lens of the keyhole.

"Who is it?" I asked.

"NYPD," the one on the left replied. They both flashed their badges and I opened the door. I stood in the doorway. They addressed me by my real name.

"That's me, officers." I said it in my nonthreatening Negro voice. "What can I do for you?" They looked like they wanted me to invite them in. I let them stay where they were.

"I'm Officer Roberts," the shorter and pudgier of the two said. His pale skin had a pinkish tinge and his close-cut hair was a dirty blond. "And this is Officer

Meadows." Meadows looked like he was probably Italian. He was about six-two, a little taller than me, and much more muscular than his shorter partner. "We want to talk to you about your assault on March twenty-sixth."

I was surprised that they hadn't turned up sooner. But I wasn't sure what to say to them.

"We've got Michael Adkins a.k.a. Mirage in custody down at the station, the man who attacked you."

Meadows peered over my shoulder at the apartment, trying to get a glimpse of what was inside. He took a quick sniff of the air like a canine. With the weed and the cable descrambler there were plenty of things he could have cuffed me for. I stood my ground to stay out of jail. Their uniforms looked extremely tight, hats too small for their meaty heads.

"Who told you it was him?" I asked. I wanted to see how much they knew, who had told them, who the witnesses were.

"We've got several witnesses who were in the building lobby at the time of the attack. A Fernando Guzman called 911 just after the incident."

"Yeah, he's the security guard," I said.

"That's right," Meadows replied. "Do you mind if we come in?"

"Well to be honest you kind of caught me at a bad time. My lady isn't decent." Carolina had actually left a half hour before. But they didn't need to know that.

"Well, we were wondering if you got a look at the men that attacked you. Maybe you could come down to the precinct and see if you can pick him out of a lineup, or look at the books."

"All I saw was three black dudes," I said, as if I hadn't seen a thing. "Then I saw stars." I gave a grin for emphasis. Roberts looked like he wanted to laugh. But he was on duty. "Once I hit the ground I just covered up."

"So you didn't see their faces at all?"

"I was on the ground covering up. When I woke up I was in the hospital."

"Why would anyone have any reason to attack you?" Roberts asked with a piercing stare.

"I heard one of them call me Allen."

Meadows jotted the name Allen down on the small pad. "Do you know any Allen's?" he asked.

"Well there's Allen Reeves," I said, knowing that I was destined to go to hell. "He writes about rappers a lot. I used to work with him. Maybe they thought I was him. I was just on my way to give some money to my friend Lamar."

"Lamar Franklin?" Meadows asked.

"Yes, he's a good friend of mine."

"He was actually the one who told us how to get in contact with you." I reminded myself to give Lamar a chop to the neck the next time I saw him.

"That was good of him. It's good to know that you

guys ask questions about this kind of thing. Wish I could help you out more though."

"So you're sure you didn't see anything? A face? Did you hear any other names?"

"I don't think so, officer," I said in my best concerned voice. "But the doctor did say that I had a concussion. Maybe it'll come back to me once I feel better."

It was plain as day that I was holding back. But no one was dead and no drugs were involved, so I was sure they had more pressing cases on their list.

"If we don't find anything soon we're going to have to release him," Roberts said. It was a final plea for me to cooperate. But it was halfhearted at best.

"Like I said, if I remember something I'll give you guys a call." I gave them both the left hand to shake and took their card. They were more than skeptical. But I was leaving it to good ole bureaucracy to make them forget all about it. And seemingly they did.

Like I said before, I wasn't sending Mirage to jail. There had to be some other way for me to settle my score, something that would drag the whole thing out into the public eye, where Mirage's label didn't want it to be. I just had to find it.

The weeks that followed flew by. Dawn followed the pitch-black darkness. Bruises and bones healed. I carefully ran in place and did leg lifts and ab raises to stay in shape. Carolina came by every few days to spend the night. Things started to feel normal again.

I'd read twelve books in six weeks, everything from *Disappearing Acts* and *Real Cool Killers* to *This Side of Paradise* and *The Jungle.* I'd also made an outline for another book, *Caution 2,* where Delante Caution and his crew find themselves taking on the Mob for control of the neighborhood drug turf. That book was going to be Dakota Grand at his finest.

"Let's go for a walk," Carolina announced one night as we were finishing up dinner.

"What?" I asked as I picked through the remainder of her shrimp enchiladas.

"I said let's go out for a walk. It's nice outside and you need to get some air in your lungs. Besides, you get your cast off on Friday. You're almost healed."

"Nah baby, I'm not goin' out until I get this thing off my arm," I said firmly. But her eyes told me that resistance was futile. She put my good arm through the sleeve of my jacket and draped the remainder over my right shoulder. It probably looked more awkward in my head than it did in reality.

"You ready?" she asked like a camp counselor on caffeine.

I sighed. "Yeah, I'm ready."

"Come on then," she said as she opened the door and closed it behind me.

We started down Clinton towards the always-busy traffic on DeKalb Avenue. She wanted to go down the hill to Fort Greene Park, even though there was no telling who or what would be lurking there under the cover of night. Like me she loved the nighttime, loved the idea of talking until the sun came up, even if it meant pure suffering during the next workday.

"So how do you feel now?" she asked just before we came to a corner. "You've been . . . quiet, since you got hurt, since that asshole jumped you."

"I'm okay," I said, trying not to return to the violent scene I'd already reviewed at least twenty times a day since it had happened. "I pretty much got everything I could ask for. I got enough money to pay the bills. I got a beautiful woman who takes care of me and I got my book comin' out soon. Fuck a broken arm and fuck Mirage." She wasn't convinced. And I definitely hadn't convinced myself.

"Sweetie, I know you really care about me but don't tell me what you think I want to hear. I know you're not done with what happened. Knowing how you hold grudges, you've probably been spending this whole time plotting some kind of revenge, some kind of way to get him back."

"What makes you say that?" I asked, playing ignorant.

"Because I know you. I know how much you want to hurt him. You want to break two arms for the one he broke on you. That's how you are, about everything. And I'm not going to tell you that you shouldn't feel that way."

"You know I don't ever think I've had a woman be that real with me," I said. I had expected her to try and discourage me the way that Maya had. We crossed Greene Avenue. A bus screeched to a halt at the red light in front of it.

"How could you?" she replied. "With the women you chose? I mean that little schoolteacher you told me about?"

"That was just one girl. They weren't all like that."

"I don't really care. I didn't have you then. But I have you now," she said, gripping my good arm tightly. I'd had to learn how to hold her all over again. "But do you think I can't figure it out, your type? You're not as hard to figure out as you think, you know?"

I'd never viewed myself as a simple personality. I wasn't the kind of guy that you just threw into a category and let him be. I had to let her know that, give her some witty retort that would stop her from believing she had me down to a science. No one did. But I couldn't come up with anything fast enough.

"Come here," I said. She stepped toward me and I

kissed her as deeply as I could, my cast arm lightly pressed against her rib cage.

"Now I've got another question."

"Do you ever run out of them?"

"You're not gonna try and go after him, are you?"

"Who?"

"Enough playing stupid, please."

"Mirage? I don't know," I said. "I don't know what I'm gonna do. I wanna do somethin' but I don't know what. This whole thing with people gettin' beat down for sayin' what they feel, the truth, has to stop. I gotta take a stand. But at the same time I don't wanna start nothing that's gonna get me killed."

"You have to figure out how you want to fight him," she said. "I don't want you getting hurt either. You men don't know when enough is enough. Whatever you do you've got to remember what's most important. Sometimes the smartest thing is to let it go."

Xiomara had said the same thing once, on the Manhattan-bound side of 125th Street station. It was well after midnight and I was still sulking that my editor at *Tango* had pulled one of my bashing club reviews because she was friends with the owner. I complained that it was unfair, that it was against the rules of pure journalism, refusing to realize that the world I covered (and was a part of) was anything but pure.

I remembered the way she rubbed the back of my

neck with her palm, instantly removing the tension and sending a rush down my spine. Her soft eyes took pity on my predicament. And though she didn't fully understand it, she was right. To let go was the best advice that she could have given me, a message from God I was trying to ignore. But out of all the emotions I could have felt, anger was the only one that registered.

Xiomara made me feel like I'd always need someone else to give me the answers. And I didn't need anybody to help me, especially when it came to the work I thought I had been made for. I had come to the Apple on my own. I didn't need her to survive. And I'd felt like I had to prove it.

A few days later I was walking down to my first apartment in Harlem, on 136th and Lenox, way before they started redeveloping it. The nameless homewrecker was sitting on my stoop, waiting for her friend (and my neighbor), who was taking her time getting out of the building. I said Hi but she acted like she didn't hear me. I made a joke about it and she laughed. I told her that she should come see me. Dressed in a cutoff T-shirt and scandalous denim shorts, she didn't exactly look like she had a crammed schedule. Purple extension braids and light brown contacts weren't the attributes of any career woman I knew. So I floated her my number and she came back like a boomerang a week later.

I told her about what I did and she had her nose wide

open. A bootleg copy of *The Matrix* ran on my thirteen-inch screen, unnoticed. We started kissing. Her hand touched my crotch. I probably heard my front door slowly creaking open, but I was distracted.

I was looking down at the back of the girl's skull as it rose and fell in a fluid motion, the tresses of her synthetic hair hanging downwards. Her talent at oral sex became more obvious by the second. But then I looked up and met my woman's rich brown eyes as they stared through the half-open doorway. Time froze. I felt the horror expressed on her face.

Xiomara moved the stare from me to the girl in my lap. And the next thing I knew a woman's boot socked Ms. X in the side of her head. She ran out in a cartoonish fashion, her limbs flailing in every direction while she made her escape. And then we had been alone, two people with three shoes between us.

Her voice tore into the frigid silence like a TV on high volume. I wanted to respond, to tell her to back off, to ask her to understand that it didn't have anything to do with her. I wanted to tell her that I was too afraid to go on, that it seemed like we were moving too fast. To me it all became in jeopardy each and every time I told her that I loved her.

But she hadn't seen any of that. What she saw was her man in another girl's mouth, her trust shattered in a million pieces on the hardwood floor. I watched as her love for me evaporate like a puddle in a heatwave. I couldn't even find a reason to try and stop her from leaving.

Everything after that had been damage control. I'd created a tightly woven mesh of lies and half-truths to keep family and friends at bay. But I decided that I never wanted to put that kind of pain on another woman's face. I didn't want to lose the best thing I ever had, again. And everything I had done since was to keep that from happening.

Carolina's lips brushed against my neck and snatched me away from the memory. My eyes were glued in the direction of the moon, just above the uniform brownstones that lined both sides of South Oxford Street. I turned to her.

"What are you looking at?" she asked. Her mocha eyes glowed in the moonlight. She rubbed her left hand against my side, where my ribs had healed, and gave me a smile that said there was nowhere else she'd rather be. After our second date she'd never asked about Xiomara again. Carolina Martinez seemed truly willing to let the past be the past, never seeming to worry that my history might repeat itself.

Just then, I didn't want to imagine living a life without her. I didn't want to wake up and not know where she was. She'd brought me out into the nighttime, in the middle of must-see TV, to show me that I'd survived, that the world outside my bunker of an apartment hadn't changed.

"The moon," I said calmly in response to her question. It was full and bright like a lit piece of china hanging in the sky.

"It's full tonight," she said. "Know what that means?"

"What?" I asked. I put my finger through a loop in her pants and pulled her close to me. She nuzzled against me like a kitten.

"Full moon means that things are going to change," she said into my chest. "You get a chance to do something over."

"Like what?" I asked.

"Whatever you didn't do right the first time."

After that night I left Xiomara and everything I felt for her where it belonged, in the past. I hoped that wherever she was she had done the same. But I had someone new to love, someone I knew better than to throw away.

We walked down to the park playground. I pushed Carolina on the swings for what seemed like hours, scanning for potential muggers and crackheads all the while. Her shapely silhouette defied gravity as it moved back and forth like a pendulum, bringing an end to the swinging confusion of a life past.

The next morning, with twenty-four hours remaining

until my cast came off, I got out of bed like a new man, early enough to see Carolina's naked behind scurry into the shower. Soon after, she covered it in her work clothes and trudged out the door announcing that she was three minutes behind schedule.

Around ten I picked up the morning paper and went down to the bodega for bread and milk. The sun touched me directly for the first time in several days and I felt more alive than I had in a long time. The *Times* said that there was a presidential debate at the Apollo Theater in Harlem and that evidence was mounting against the four cops in the Diallo case up in Albany. According to them the defense's own witnesses had turned against them. That made a good day even better.

It was 10:25 when I came back up Clinton Avenue towards my building. Someone was waiting for me and I hadn't been expecting any guests. He was a shirt-and-tied white boy in his late twenties who was balding at the temples. I'd never seen him on the block or in the neighborhood. But since I'd been house-ridden for weeks I assumed that he'd recently joined the area's current efforts to flush all people of color another ten blocks east.

"Mr. Grand?" he asked uncertainly.

"Yeah," I said, fearing nothing but death and the approaching tax deadline.

"Hi, I'm Ben Kaufield. I'm a staff writer for the New

York *Daily News* and I was wondering if I could ask you some questions."

I wanted to ask him how he'd found me. But the answer was simple enough. I was in the phone book. My address was listed.

"About what?"

"About your incident with the rapper Mirage and why as yet you haven't pressed charges. I tried calling, but I kept getting busy signals."

"I didn't think you guys would think it was important." If the press was involved I knew that Roberts and Meadows would definitely be coming back. And they'd probably bring the DA with them.

"We report the news," he said seriously. "And this is news, Mr. Grand."

"You can call me D. Come on up."

Inside I situated myself on the sofa, the aging cast in my lap. He planted his tape recorder on the coffee table and pressed record. He sat in the ratty vinyl recliner I'd found in front of the building the day I moved in. It was strange having the mic pointed in my direction.

"This whole story came about because I like rap," he said, as if I needed convincing. "I listen to the music and I like a lot of the things that it has to say. But this story isn't about music. It's about a form of extortion."

"What do you mean?" I asked.

"Tell me if I'm wrong. But it goes like this: You do an

exposé on an artist. He doesn't like it, so you get put in the hospital. Don't you think that sends a message to other journalists, that if they rock an artist's boat they're going to be hurt?"

I was cautious about what I was going to say. But he seemed to be humming my tune perfectly. I knew that he could only print my exact words, even if he changed them around for dramatic effect. But just then something popped into my mind: Kaufield could be the perfect vehicle for my Mirage retribution.

He could give me the weapon I needed to destroy Mirage. And I'd never have to look at him, much less touch him. Millions read the *Daily News* every morning. So whatever I said and he wrote could cover the city's surface like snow before a day's end.

"It definitely does," I replied sternly. "I'm the third journalist in the last few months. This is becoming a pattern and it's one that has to stop."

"And how do you stop something like this?"

"Someone has to take a stand," I said. "Someone has to make an example of these artists, let them know that we're not going to be stepped on, make a change in this game of an industry that we work in."

"It's interesting that you say that," Kaufield interjected. "I've already talked to both Walt Wilson and Tyrone Fields. They seemed to dismiss it as just something that happens, as if they're used to it." I felt a surge of pride for not taking that check from GQ Smooth back at the hospital.

"You can't blame them," I said. "When we got into this game we just wanted to do our part for the music. We're the only ones there to say everything the Establishment doesn't about hip-hop. So when something like this happens I think the natural response, for the sake of the music and the artist, is to just let it all roll down your back. We're all alive. Injuries heal."

"But you're not taking that route?"

"No, I'm not. This kind of thing isn't acceptable. There are consequences and repercussions for these violent actions. And while I couldn't put Mirage behind bars, because I didn't actually see him, I'm going to do what I can to make my presence felt in his life."

"What do you mean by that?"

"I'm doing my part by talking to you," I said as my voice increased in volume. "This thing is out in the open now. I mean I was the biggest Arbor Day fan on the planet. I *bought* all the albums and all the bootleg studio dubs and B-sides. When I was seventeen I threw a drink in some kid's face just so I could snatch the Arbor Day towel he'd caught off of the stage. They were everything to me and it took me five years to get my first interview with them, and that was three weeks after they broke up. Then I go on the interview and Mirage is telling me things no one has ever heard before, things that could help the fans understand why the breakup happened.

"So those were the things I wrote about in the article. I thought I had done something monumental, for him and his fans. Then a few months later he says I made it all up because he was high, then brutally assaults me and puts me in the hospital. I've spent six weeks sitting in this apartment with a concussion, a broken arm, and fractured ribs, wondering if I would ever be the same, if I could still protect and defend the music the same way I used to."

"So you didn't see his face at all during the attack?"

"No," I said, the lie continuing to squeeze through my teeth. "Besides, I've never gone running to the police to settle a disagreement in my life. And I'm not going to start now. He and I will cross paths when the time is right."

I stopped there. I could have said much more but I knew I'd given Kaufield more than he could use. I figured that by morning the word would be out to half the city that I wasn't going out like a chump on this thing, that it wasn't over, and that I wasn't just doing it for myself, but for all of us.

"What do you hope that the two of you 'crossing paths' would accomplish?" Kaufield asked.

"I don't know. But when it happens I'll feel a lot better."

I gave Kaufield a stone-faced expression for several seconds. Then he stopped his tape.

"Wow, well I guess that's about it. If I have any questions is there a way I can get ahold of you?"

"Just call me here," I said. "I know you have the number if you have my address."

He gave me a slight grin as he slipped his recorder into his right front pocket and slipped his pen through the rings at the top of his reporter's notebook.

"Very good," he said. We shook and I walked him to the door. I'd given him a story. But he was the one who had to write it. Maybe it would be *his* breakthrough piece.

He called me back two days later to tell me that the story would run the following Wednesday. It bothered me that I had to wait that long to see if my mousetrap would work.

My physician, Dr. Olayemi, West African medical expatriate extraordinaire, removed my cast and replaced it with brown gauze and a brace. He said it had healed perfectly in less time than it took many. I told him that I had always been an extraordinary healer and he enjoyed a long chuckle.

"If you were that extraordinary it wouldn't have been broken in the first place."

Just then I wanted to sick the INS on him. But he was the only choice with my HMO.

Plaster-free for the first time in almost two months, I enjoyed a Newport and a shot of Hennessy at a dive bar on the corner of 119th and Adam Clayton Powell. I didn't even look at the name of the place as I walked in.

The mirrors behind the bar were so warped that my face looked like a reflection from a fun house. The small scars on my right cheek were now two thin parallel lines. The vitamin E and cocoa butter had helped. But just looking at them in my exaggerated reflection brought Mirage back into focus.

"Man, that nigga gon' get his tonight," a voice yelled at the other end of the bar. Or had the words come from inside of my own head? I took a puff from my square and cut my eyes to the right. A few stools down were two men in lined bubble coats and T-shirts drinking Heinekens. They both seemed older than me, their hair in prison cornrows, platinum chains with crucifixes swinging from their necks.

"Nah man, don't even go out like that," the other argued. "You got a little shorty now. You can't be startin' a beef wit' every nigga on the block like you used to." There was a pause of contemplation followed by a change of topic. Ten minutes later they whisked themselves into the street like paper in the wind.

I mulled over the words they'd spoken and figured out that their story was all too clichéd. I knew it because I'd lived it. And when I didn't live it I'd seen it lived by those around me, back at home.

The loud one had been the aging homeboy who'd lived the thug life for so long that he'd never learned what being a man was all about. Now, because he'd gotten some girl pregnant he had to start making the right choices. After a beer and good advice from a wise and more level-headed friend he was now headed into the streets of Harlem having learned a lesson about what was important. He was "doing the right thing." They always made that so simple in the movies, and on TV. In reality, determining what was *right* was a lot more complicated.

With the *Daily News* article I thought I was setting the stage for something big, something beyond the post-party talks we had about artists and execs making threats and giving beatdowns. The whole champagne bottle thing with Puffy had been a milestone. But the internal gum-flapping never went anywhere. That was why I couldn't wait for Kaufield's article to come out.

I imagined the look on Mirage's face after he read it. I wanted to know the first words that came out of his mouth after he finished the last sentence. Even after Maya's and Carolina's good advice I was still obsessed. I needed someone to talk me off of the ledge, to help me level my head. But there was no one that could have forced me to listen. It was one of the many times that I wished I had a real father to call.

I usually didn't miss him. He had always been less of dad and more of Mama's occasional live-in boyfriend. The more I knew my mother the more I understood why their thing worked. She needed someone who did what she told him to do and my father was the kind of person that liked to take instructions. He didn't put up any static in the house because he had enough to worry about out in the streets. The similarities between us began and ended with our eyes and build, irises the color of cognac, medium shoulders and slim waists.

He spent most of his time in front of the TV, drinking E&J mixed with Pepsi and smoking Lucky Strikes a pack at a time. He was a man of the streets, the kind of dime-store hustler everybody has at least one of in their family. Once, just before my last year of high school, he had told me that college was a waste of my time and that I was in too much of a hurry to get out in the world. He promised that the world was ready and waiting to eat me alive.

I hated him for that. I'd hated him for making my mother work too many hours trying to make up for his need to do things his way. But the good thing was that he had made me inadvertently push myself harder and harder. No matter what I did I had to at least get past where he was. He was also why I called Mama a hypocrite. She'd had the nerve to curse me for leaving school but had spent too much of her life laying up with a career criminal who paid bills by pawning the neighbors' stolen TVs and silverware.

I remember at age ten when we all had to go down to the emergency room so that my father could get his jaw wired. He'd gotten hit with a pipe after being caught trying to break into somebody's house by trying to pick the lock with a credit card. He said he'd seen it on TV and thought that it might work. He drank his dinner for almost three months.

With Pop out of the picture I'd never had anyone to look up to but myself, the only boy in a family of matriarchs: aunts, cousins, and widowed grandmothers with similar experiences. At least that clichéd punk at the bar had a kid to look after. If I died my legacy would vanish like a deleted paragraph.

■ ■ ■

As FAR AS Carolina was concerned, having no cast meant that I'd run out of excuses for not going out. The ribs and arm were back to normal. The light-headedness when I stood up was mostly gone. So in a three-day period we had dinner at Café Lafayette, we went to see *Next Friday* at the Plaza Twin, and there was a wedding that Saturday.

I'd been to two weddings in my life, both of which were before my fourteenth birthday. Both times my mother had made me put on my secondhand Easter suit, a short-sleeved white shirt, and my only tie, a black clip-on. Almost a decade later at twenty-two, I still didn't own a single suit. And Carolina had no intentions of letting me get by with my slightly undersized blazer and a pair of khakis.

So she towed me to the Brooks Brothers on 33rd Street in search of something respectable.

I never liked to dress up. There was something about tight collars and jackets with lapels that made my stomach queasy. Those clothes reminded me of long church services and hard wood pews that made my behind sore. My last suit had come and gone with high school, as had church. But now, with Carolina twisting one arm behind my back, I had to purchase a new suit, shirts, and at least two ties.

"Do you know how to match?" she asked from behind her dark diva shades as the store came into view.

"What, you think I'm color-blind?"

"I didn't ask you if you could see colors. I asked if you could match them. There's a big difference."

"I hope you tryin' to be funny."

"I'm just asking a very important question, papi."

"Yes Carolina, I do know how to match colors."

"I believe you, D. But before we even go in here I'm going to tell you one thing."

"What's that?"

"I'm picking out the suit and the shirts and the ties. You are going to behave, try things on when I ask you to, and not give me any problems."

"Okay. I guess you're trying to take control here."

"I already have it, sweetie," she said with a slick grin.

"And who told you that?"

"C'mon, D. We don't have time to stroke your ego. I'm wearing the pants right now."

"All I see is a gray skirt."

"I love you too much to argue with you. Just go inside the store, stupid." She gave my wrist a strong tug and pulled me across the street. She had said the three magic words and part of me froze, wondering if I would ever have the courage to repeat them.

On the other side of the entrance she turned into the Afro-Cuban Donna Karan as she requested measuring tape and a scale to measure my shoe size.

"We're gettin' shoes too?"

"D, what did I say outside?" With that warning I said no more, still pondering the three words she had uttered.

In minutes I learned that I still wore a size 38 jacket and 34×32 pants. My shoe size was still an 11 and I had a 14½" neck. We went through every shade of black and dark blue in search of the suit that would bring my ordeal to a stop. After the first thirty minutes our salesman, a blond stick figure in his early forties, looked like she'd been smacking him around for an hour. I truly sympathized.

But after almost two hours she finally settled on a single-breasted charcoal-black ensemble and a twin version in navy blue. My new shoes were Rockport wing tips (painfully pointed at the toe) and she'd picked two solid white Egyptian cotton shirts. The ties alone were almost $75 so I didn't want to think about how much I was spending for everything else.

"One of those should work for the reception," she said upon further examining the neckpieces.

"The reception? What about the wedding?"

"We're just going to the reception. This is just my friend from work. It isn't like she's going to be looking for us when she's coming down the aisle."

"So basically we went through the last two hours just so I could look good at a party? Damn, you been actin' like I was in the wedding."

"Sweetie, I can't have my man looking like a homeless person anywhere I'm going," she said playfully. "I have a reputation, you know?"

"A reputation for makin' things a lot harder than they need to be."

"D, you have three things you're good at—writing,

cooking, and keeping me entertained. I'll handle all fashion, okay?"

"This ain't gonna be no white wedding is it?"

"You've been to my office," she said matter-of-factly as we descended into the station for the D train. "Of course it is."

Two days later we were chocolate specks on a huge vanilla napkin. The walls, tablecloths, and even the cake were all absent of color. Carolina worked the room while I repeatedly dodged trite conversations on my way to and from the bar. I felt ten pounds heavier after three hits of Hennessy. That was just when the bride and groom awkwardly made their way to the center of the dance floor.

The band went into an artless medley that probably had all of the dead Motown greats turning in their graves. Fifteen minutes later they were on to pseudo-salsa. Carolina dragged my sluggish frame onto the dance floor. I was pretty buzzed but I held my own, moving my feet the way she'd shown me on countless occasions. It didn't take long before we were gliding on air.

"You're really special, you know that?" she asked as the song faded out.

"And why am I so special?" I asked, waiting for one of her usual punch lines.

"Because most black guys can't dance salsa, or least not as well as you. Plus you're sooo cute."

"Like you ain't black," I replied.

"I'm not. I'm a Cuban of African descent."

"Whatever."

She touched my face. The warmth from her hand crept through me like a good buzz. I pulled her close and kissed her like it was the last time I could.

This time I didn't have to fight the words. They rose to the top of my throat like foam in root beer. And I smiled.

"I love you," I said plainly. She looked at me for a moment, through my eyes and into something I didn't even know was there. Maya had said that someone would come along who took you somewhere else. If there had been doubt at the park that night, now I *knew* that she was it.

"Let's go home," she whispered with urgency.

What transpired on my mattress an hour afterwards changed my life. For the first time ever I made *love* to her. And when it was over, I, we, were something different, and I was ready for what was ahead.

■ ■ ■

"YOU SHOULD COME to Cuba," she announced sometime after dawn the next morning. "You'd like it."

194

"I guess I'll have to do that sometime, like when the State Department doesn't send you to jail for getting on the plane."

"Like you always follow the rules. Anyway I'm serious. You should go sometime, sometime soon." She sounded surprisingly anxious about it at a time in the morning when I barely knew where I was, not to mention when the next time would be that I could take a trip out of the country.

"We can take a bus to Canada and fly out for under seven hundred dollars. And we'd stay with my parents. They live near the beach, at least they did the last time I saw them. I haven't been there in so long, not since I finished school. And I send everything through my uncle in the DR."

"How come you didn't go back before you came here?"

"Because I'm the only girl in the family and I'm also the oldest. So I wanted to come back with something, something other than a husband, which is about the only thing my family expects. When I go back I want to have proof that I made something of myself here."

"So what's there to do in Cuba?"

"There aren't as many little comforts as here. There isn't cable TV or a lot of designer clothes or anything like that. It's very poor. But the thing about home is that you can be you, no matter who you are."

"You make it sound like it's Fantasy Island or something."

"No, if it was paradise then I'd still be there now, wouldn't I?" Her silhouette blocked the scant morning sun rays streaming through the bedroom window.

"But you'd like it there. I know you would."

"I think I would too," I said, imagining standing on a beach in front of crystal-blue water, my woman holding one arm, a joint in the other. That would have truly been the way to enjoy life.

We spent the rest of the day in bed. In the morning I got up and ran down to the diner on Lafayette and grabbed breakfast and the Sunday paper. She read technology and travel. I clipped coupons and read the entertainment and the comics. Before we knew it it was dark again. She had to go home because she'd forgotten to bring a change of clothes. I put her in a cab just before ten and stood on the sidewalk in sweatpants and slippers as the car took her back towards Crown Heights.

■ ■ ■

THAT NIGHT, AS I slept, I returned to the bar where Mirage and I had previously met. All the glasses on the bar were black and dirty, even the one in front of me, which was filled to the brim with vodka, my least favorite spirit.

"I can't stand this job," he said.

"Why?" I asked calmly as I took a sip from the grimy glass.

"Because I have to serve everybody. I even have to serve you."

"What's wrong with serving me?"

"You can't make up your mind. So I gotta keep doin' it over and over again."

There was a long silence and the scene faded to black. I woke up with only traces of remembrance.

I slowly began to lose the fear that my healing bone was going to break with the slightest touch. I'd followed the doctor's orders for the whole six weeks about not doing anything strenuous, I hadn't even used that arm to wipe the sweat off my brow. But hunger made me push the envelope. Instead of ordering out I decided to cook. I had to get into the habit of cooking again. And as I stirred pots and raised flames an idea came into focus.

After the food was done I ran to my laptop and tried to make sense out of the vague idea. My fingers hovered over the keyboard, but nothing came out. I was like an open faucet with pressure turned off. I closed my eyes and tried to relax.

"You better do something," Mirage had chided behind my eyelids. I typed his quote as the first words for *Caution* 2. The other sentences followed.

It didn't take me long to get my hero, Delante Caution, back into blood, broads, and bullets. I wrote the shootouts and beatdowns with razor-sharp accuracy, all the while making it clear that this was a guy who didn't take any shit. That was the way I was, or at least the way I was going to be from then on. When I was done I had twenty pages to show for my work. The night ended in a dreamless sleep as I anxiously awaited the coming of a new day.

■ ■ ■

IT WAS *THE* Wednesday. I jumped out of bed and into my sweatshirt and house shoes. Two minutes later I was at my doorstep. But when I got there my *Daily News* was nowhere to be found. Mike, one of my upstairs neighbors, had a bad habit of *borrowing* my paper whenever he felt like it and today he'd walked off with the most important installment of my three-month trial subscription. But I wasn't going to throw a tantrum about it.

So I jogged down Clinton to the bodega on Gates and St. James, picked up three copies, and jogged them back to the house before I began reading.

I licked my lips as I began to scan the headlines. I was about to get my revenge the right way, by expressing my feelings in a public forum, making a statement and a stand in just the way that writers were supposed to. Soon all of New York would know the truth about Mirage and me. I found the article and began to read.

Kaufield's lead paragraph was interesting, something about the codependent relationship between stars and the media. Then he put in the grabber sentence about what happens when that relationship causes one to attack the other. I skimmed for four paragraphs until I found my name.

Dakota Grand, an up-and-coming journalist for publications such as *Maintain*, *The Source* and most recently *The Magazine*, is recovering at home after an attack at the hands of rapper/producer Mirage, formerly a member of the hit group Arbor Day. Mirage, along with two other men, allegedly attacked Grand in the lobby of 235 Lexington Avenue, after a disagreement over an article Grand had written on him and his former partner. Grand has suffered a broken arm, fractured ribs, a concussion and several other injuries but has declined to press charges because he was unable to positively ID his attackers. However, other eyewitnesses placed the rapper at the scene with several other men. But every witness was conveniently uncertain as to who actually took part in the assault. "I've never gone running to the police to settle a disagreement in my life," Grand said angrily when asked about taking additional legal action. "He and I will cross paths when the time is right. And I'll be ready."

It was just like a reporter to cut everything I said down to the last two lines. The next two paragraphs were crammed with spineless quotes from the other victims who said they were willing to let the whole thing go and stay out of court. I knew that they'd all taken the money. My name turned up again in a later paragraph:

When asked about the situation with Dakota Grand at the video shoot for his solo debut single "Smoke and Mirrors," Mirage accused Grand of exaggerating the claims in his statements. "For legal reasons I can't speak on the incident. But I will say that Mr. Dakota should stick to writing and stop acting. He's trying to take this thing to a level that he can't afford for it to go."

The paper hit the floor like a brick. I'd shot and missed. Plus I'd been misquoted. The city would now see me as some wannabe tough guy who couldn't leave well enough alone and go back to work. Now, as a result of poor journalism, I'd be the laughingstock of the industry before the end of the day.

I panicked. The whole thing was escalating. I had to get out of town, change my name, move to Cuba with Carolina. Mirage would be out there, waiting to hunt me down like an animal, both articles balled in each fist.

Then I derailed that train of thought. I was going overboard. He was *not* looking for me. I should have been more angry that a white boy came all the way out to Brooklyn to use two sentences from a half hour of tape. He'd printed just enough to make me look like a joke. I had to call him and let him know how disappointed I was with his journalistic abilities, maybe even head up to his office and pay him a visit. I reached for the phone and it rang. A lot of that had been happening lately.

"Yeah?" I answered.

"You need to watch what you write, muthafucka!" The voice was deep and breathy, as if the person had just run the 100-meter dash. "You shoulda got me locked up when you had the fuckin' chance!"

"Who is this?" I asked. I knew but I didn't want to believe it. I should have spent the extra money to keep my number unlisted.

"I think you know who it is, *Da*-kota Grand. You got a lot of mouth don't you?" He laughed to himself. "But I done already stomped your ass. Even tried to give you some money for it. Now I'm just gonna give you some advice. You can't battle me all by yourself. Keep fuckin' around wit' Mirage and I'll send your head home in a box." There was a flash of static and I got a dial tone.

This time it hadn't been one of my bartender nightmares. My left leg began to tremble uncontrollably as I sat down. My nerves were so gone that it was a struggle to put the phone down in the cradle. Someone must have sold me out, led him right to me. Lamar? Maya? Massai Morris? Allen Reeves? Who could it have been? But accusing people wasn't going to change the matter at hand. He'd said he was going to send my head home in a box. I was going to be decapitated, dismembered, murdered.

I tried to stand up but the trembling leg wouldn't hold me. It folded under the weight and I slipped back onto the futon. I breathed in and out slowly, trying to rationalize what had just happened. I had taken a stand and now he was trying to take my life. I had to do something.

But Mirage was right. I was only one man, and one smaller than him at that. Going up against him meant going up against bodyguards, armed felons, attorneys, and A&R executives. He seemed untouchable. But so did every rap star, until someone, something, or a really bad record brought them down.

DAKOTA GRAND

■ ■ ■

My muscles got ahold of themselves. There was no room for fear. The phone rang again. I thought of not answering. But I picked up before the machine on the fourth ring. It was Lamar.

"I'm not even gonna ask if you read the paper today." He was the last person I could tell about what had just transpired.

"You know I did," I said.

"Everybody's talkin' about it here. I even had my boy out in LA call and ask me about it. So what you gonna do?"

Wasn't it obvious? Couldn't he see where I was headed?

"What do you mean what am I gonna do?"

"I'd suggest you lay low for a while," he said in a lowered tone of voice. The door to his glass cubicle must have been open.

"What the hell am I gonna lay low for?" I said loudly. I wanted my voice to carry through his earpiece. I wanted all those weak hip-hop rats in the background to know what was about to go down. "You think I'm scared of him?"

"He put you in the hospital the last time," he muttered. "Word is he's losing more of his mind by the minute. I know you ain't tryin' to get that same arm broke again."

"Yeah he put me in the hospital. So what?" I said, trying to sound indestructible. "But that was when he had two of his boys with him. And I put his nuts in his stomach before I went down too."

"That ain't the point, man. You got way more to lose than him. You got a career, a girl, a book deal. Man, he's just a rapper. Rappers come and go, man. Sooner than you think he'll be waiting in line to get in the club like everybody else." Mirage had been in the game ten years and that still hadn't happened.

"You don't understand, man," I said, desperation in my voice. "It goes deeper than that."

"Man, you need to calm down. You need to *calm down*. You sound like you're goin' as crazy as he is."

"The last thing I am is crazy!"

I hung up the phone without a goodbye and knew that he wouldn't call back. A friend would have left work to come over. A friend would have said we needed to have a drink to talk about it. But all Lamar would do was call someone else and keep the rumor mill turning. The real friends in my life were in short supply.

Laying low was out, especially now that he knew my phone number. That meant he probably had the address too. He could kick my door in whenever he wanted.

And what if Carolina was there when it happened? Or even Maya? I couldn't let them get caught in the middle.

But I wasn't sure if I could afford the price of the action I wanted to take. I knew what needed to be done but this was the first time that I'd had to do it. I had a clean police record, no speeding tickets. Worry and concern screamed in my ears like annoying children. But all it took was a flash of what I looked like when I first woke up in the hospital, a mental Polaroid of my leg shaking violently from just his phone call, and like Delante Caution, I wasn't going to take any more of his shit. I decided to declare a war.

■　■　■

I PITCHED MY cigarette out of the cab's rear window just before it stopped in East Flatbush, about ten blocks away from the site of my first meeting with Mirage. Day had turned to night. But it was still almost 70 degrees, too warm for the leather jacket and T-shirt I was wearing. I wiped my brow with my stolen Arbor Day commemorative towel. In the other hand was a pint of Hennessy, from which I had swigged continuously for the duration of the car trip. But I had to save some, for later.

I had the cabbie drop me off far enough away to avoid suspicion, if the cops were to ask cab radio dispatchers about fares in Flatbush the morning after. I figured that ten blocks was too far of a distance to connect me to anything.

I reveled in the calm the nicotine gave me. I'd tried to quit smoking for Carolina. But the death threats and assaults had more than worn down my willpower. Life under pressure was impossible without Newports.

I passed through blocks of dark buildings and run-down storefronts. Men and women whisked by en route to their nighttime destinations. Back in Atlanta I could have heard a pin drop at 3 a.m. on a Tuesday. But like big brother Manhattan, Brooklyn rarely slept.

Carolina didn't have a clue about what I was doing. Earlier in the night I'd called and told her that I was writing and needed to get some things out of my head. She told me that was fine as long as I promised to have lunch with her the next day. I yessed her off the phone because time was of the essence.

The studio came into view and the first thing I saw was the same blue 4.6 Range Rover that had been parked there on the day of the interview. It had to be Mirage's. He'd mentioned Ranges more than enough times in his lyrics. And seeing the parked truck confirmed my suspicion that he was there.

The latest gossip from the websites was that Mirage's record label was pressuring him to finish the last few songs for the album since the single, "Smoke and Mirrors," was doing so well on radio. I also read between the lines that with all of his crazy behavior, they were trying to get it all done just in case some jail time was on its way down the pipe. All of that translated into him having to do more than a few all-nighters at the studio. So he'd left his precious $60,000-plus automobile outside and defenseless.

I knew I only had about twenty seconds if there was an alarm. I removed the flathead screwdriver from my jacket pocket. I placed it in the tiny space around the fuel tank opening. I waited for something to go off. But nothing happened. He must have only had a kill switch, maybe Lo-Jack. I pried open the tank and removed the cap. Then I took that commemorative towel, soaked it with the remainder of the Hennessy, and stuffed it down into the tank. I lit the tail end of the liquor-soaked fabric with my lighter and then Michael Johnsoned down the street.

The boom hit before I had passed the first two buildings next to the studio. A second, louder explosion followed. The ground shook beneath me. I wanted to stop and watch but avoiding prosecution and/or death took priority. I turned right at the corner and slowed to a normal walking pace, which I continued for seven blocks. Then I turned left and headed towards the nearest No. 2 station, where I waited forty-five minutes in the middle of the night just to travel three stops. I wiped off both the lighter and the cognac bottle and deposited them in a trash can on the subway platform just before the train whisked me back to Eastern Parkway station. I walked another twelve blocks home. Mission accomplished.

I reentered my apartment with an evil grin. But my conscience quickly wiped it away. Had someone been in the car? Had the studio caught fire? Of course not. I had gotten away. Mirage would now know that I was the one writer he'd better not fuck with.

But fear was perched on my eyelids when I got up six hours later. I had a throbbing headache and had somehow pulled a muscle in my right shoulder. I had acted out what seemed like a perfect plan the night before, only to wake up with the painfully obvious—that I would be at the top of the suspect list. Sure the cops like Roberts and Meadows were racist pigs that were dumber than goldfish. But my case would have been all too easy.

Mirage's car had blown up the night after an article ran in the second-largest paper in the city, where it could have been interpreted that I directly swore revenge on the man. They could have also checked my phone records and found the call he'd made to my house. And upon investigation they could have seen that there had been nothing to stop me from going down to the studio and setting off the explosion. The only thing in my favor was that there couldn't have been too many witnesses at four in the morning.

It was also in my favor that the mainstream was convinced that all rappers were gun-toting ex-thugs who were constantly in paranoid fear of their lives and possessions. Most important the cops weren't going to bend over backwards for a rapper who'd made more than his share of public comments against the NYPD in the past few years.

Had I been covering the story I would have used all of those facts to prove the wrongs of the Rotten Apple's justice system. But I wasn't covering it. I *was* the story. And I felt like I was drenched in guilt, despite the flimsiness of their potential case. My feet weren't even on the bedroom floor before my mind was plagued with daymares of a courtroom sentencing and stabbing inmates to survive during my bid upstate for reckless endangerment and destruction of private property.

I needed an alibi and the 4 a.m. rerun of *Midnight Love* on BET wasn't going to do it. But who could vouch for me? Carolina was the obvious candidate. But I didn't want her involved or aware that when I'd said I was writing I was really setting off explosions in another part of Brooklyn.

I thought of Maya but she was still out of town. Lamar was next on the alibi ballot. Then I quickly remembered that duck tape couldn't keep his mouth shut. But counting him out meant that I didn't have anyone else to ask. But there was one other person.

He would be familiar with my dilemma and would know how to take immediate action. I dialed his pager number from memory and he called back forty minutes later, just after I had begun to pick at the chipping paint on the bedroom windowsill.

"Yo, this is T!" he yelled into the phone with the sounds of horns and passing traffic in the background.

"Yeah man, it's D!"

"Yo wassup son? Where you been at the last couple of months? I got some songs I did that I want you to hear."

"I just been busy, man," I replied nervously. "But look, I need to talk to you about somethin' and I don't wanna do it over the phone."

"Well I'm up in the Bronx right now. I usually ain't up this early but I just came from this girl's house. See her man gets back at—well anyway I'll be back at my crib in forty-five minutes. You wanna meet me there?"

"Yeah. What's the address again?"

"1510 128th Street. It's 128th and Lenox, number three."

"Cool. I'll be there in like an hour and a half."

As I hung up the phone, I hadn't anticipated making a run to Harlem first thing in the morning. But nailing down an alibi was crucial. I wanted to have my official story together even before I read the paper to see what page the explosion story had landed on. I was out of the house by eleven-thirty and to the train by a quarter to twelve. On the way I got a coffee, a cranberry muffin, and, of course, the *Daily News*. But as the 4 train pulled away from Atlantic Avenue I realized that the story I was looking for was nowhere to be found.

I'd imagined the headline in huge block lettering: "Rapper's Range Rover Destroyed in Explosion" or "Arbor Day Suffers Forest Blaze." But when I got to the article I let out a sigh of disbelief. I had missed, again.

There was no blaring large-print headline, only a tiny blurb in the Metro section. The lead read:

Flatbush, Brooklyn—The explosion of a Jeep at Brooklyn's Chocolate Fudge studios has neighborhood residents concerned about the resurgence of gang violence in the area.

The remaining sentences went on to say that the explosion had been attributed to rising tensions between the studio's owners and neighborhood crime lords who were angered by the owner's refusal to allow them to use the facilities to record a demo tape they were working on. There was even a quick quote from one of the managers, Flynt Hamlin, who corroborated the whole thing, including the fact that the Range Rover was his. I'd blown up the wrong person's jeep by mistake.

That was when I finally remembered that Mirage didn't have a driver's license. He'd alluded to the fact in numerous interviews, all of which I'd read numerous times. How could I have forgotten that? I must have been losing my mind.

In light of the paper's new information, I wasn't exactly sure what I was going to talk to TD about. But I'd already set up a meeting and I didn't want to stand him up. I always kept my meetings. Besides, it wouldn't hurt to visit the man. He'd been inviting me up for more than a year and I had yet to make it once.

Short on sleep, I closed my eyes for most of the ride. I wanted to drift away from the drama of the moment and move to a warm beach with a huge sand castle and the beautiful waves toppling the structure. But I didn't travel to that place. Instead I found myself in a daydream version of my mother's basement, the way I remembered it looking when I lived down there back in high school, just after we'd moved out of the projects. I was down there watching Mirage's face on a television screen. Then I was up in front of the idiot box trying to kick the screen in. But my foot couldn't crack the glass. I opened my eyes and quickly returned to the train's dingy scenery, a dull headache above my temples.

The walk to TD's apartment from the train was longer than I'd expected, but I needed the time to figure out what my new "urgent" news for TD was going to be about. I could have told him that I'd met a producer who was looking for artists and that I needed a copy of his demo tape. But he knew I would have said that over the phone without a problem. There were plenty of things I could have said. But by the time I got to his building I was set on just telling him the truth.

"Wassup yo!" he yelled before the door was even completely open. He snatched me into a quick hug and dragged me over the threshold. "It's been like forever."

"Yeah," I replied.

As he closed the door I saw that his apartment was barely wider than the subway car I'd just left. The place strained to fit the twin bed at the far end, a love seat, and a coffee table with two chairs and a 15-inch color TV, the room's centerpiece. Adorning the sofa was a sleeve-less-T-shirted kid who shared TD's long nose and full lips.

"Well, this is it!" T said. "My philosophy is you make 'em think you down and out while you really puttin' all your money into gettin' rich." The nameless figure on the sofa shook his head in silent doubt of T's statement.

"I hear you," I said blankly as I scanned the empty wall space that spread through the apartment like a disease. I

had to wonder if he really had any money invested anywhere. It wasn't the kind of place you lived in just because you wanted to save your cake.

The kid on the couch was introduced as his little
brother Sam. Sam was staying with him until he gradu-
ated from high school and could find his own small and
narrow apartment. Looking at the kid more closely I noticed the tattoo on his left shoulder of a bullet passing
through an exploding heart. Generation Y. After being
introduced, Sam gave me a quick nod and started up a
game of NBA Live on the PlayStation system in front of
the television.

In the next few minutes TD offered me a chair from
the coffee table, a Heineken from the otherwise empty
half-refrigerator, and a puff from the blunt he'd freshly
rolled atop his latest issue of *Black Tail* magazine. I politely declined them all.

"So what you need?" he asked with his eyes focused
on the burning stick in his right hand. "I know you need
somethin' because of that look you got on your face."

"What look?"

"The look that says you done messed somethin' up
and you need somebody like me to help you fix it."

I hadn't expected him to be that direct. But I did need
something from him, and it was the first time I'd ever
asked. He'd spent most of our exchanges thanking me
for tickets or passes or introductions to people who

probably wouldn't return his calls. Now he had to pay me back. This just happened to be a favor I thought my life depended on.

"Well, you know Mirage, right?"

"Nah," he replied sarcastically. "I don't know the dude that made me want to start rappin'." TD was the last person I needed to be an Arbor Day fan.

"You like him that much?"

"Nah, I started rappin' 'cuz I knew I could beat his punk ass."

I sighed in relief as inconspicuously as I could.

"Well, you remember when I did that piece on him?"

"Yeah, the one in *The Magazine?*"

"Yeah, well he didn't like the piece so he jumped me, stomped me out and broke my arm and ribs." I pointed to the newly healed limb for emphasis.

He looked at my arm and then into my eyes, which he studied intently to see if I was joking. Then his lips made a grin that burst into a loud laugh.

"That was you?" he asked with a chuckle. "Yo Sam, this was the one Mirage beat the shit out of. Remember when Davon up the block told us about that?"

"Him?" Sam asked his big brother as he paused his game and walked toward us. "Davon made it seem like he was a little scrawny muthafucka."

"Yeah man, I heard about it and I wondered if it was you," T said just as Sam came over and leaned on his brother's shoulder with a forearm. "But I didn't think you'd go out like that."

It was one thing to know that the media had picked up the story. But I'd fallen into the very depths of shame knowing that my demise was in the mouth of every young black man on the street. To my supposed peers, I looked weak for letting it happen at all. That added an entirely new dimension to what I had to do.

"Before you start laughin' you better know that I didn't just fall on the ground and get stomped," I said proudly. "I kicked Mirage in the nuts and clocked one of his boys straight in the grille before I went down."

"I can respect that," the two said, almost in unison.

"So what else happened?" T probed.

"Well I was up in my house for a while while my arm was in a cast. And this reporter was doin' a story on the whole thing. So I dissed Mirage in the interview. But when I read the story I saw that he'd made me look like I was fakin'. Then he called me and said he was gon' kill me. So to make a long story short I went down to the studio where he was supposed to be at and I lit a rag in the gas tank and blew up his jeep. But today I found out that it wasn't even his jeep. So now I need you to help me to think of a way to get some real payback."

Before I had even finished, the look on Sam's face read total and complete disgust. He chimed in first.

"Payback? Nigga, this ain't no Mel Gibson movie. You

got beef with somebody you handle it. And not by blowin' up cars like somebody's stalker ass girlfriend. You catch him at the club with some boys and stomp him out. Or you jig him in the gut right when he's comin' backstage from a show. And if you got to you pull a trigger and put some heat in him. That's it. There ain't no plan to come up with. Fuck a plan."

Sam then returned to the couch to finish his game. I was still standing by the door.

"For once my little brother said it better than I would," TD remarked. His spliff was now half of its previous length. "You wanna make him hurt, you make him hurt. You look him in the eye the same way he did you and you make him remember what he did to you. That's what you wanna do and that's why you here."

Silence hung in the air for a breath's time. I was a writer, a scribe. Before the article and the death threat and the explosion all I had wanted was some respect, for him to admit that he was wrong, maybe just an apology, and not even a public one at that.

But now an "I'm sorry" was about as likely as a winning lottery ticket. He was going to send my head home to Atlanta in a box. There had been both daydreams and nightmares, chronic flashbacks from being beaten into a marble floor. None of it was going away. I had to do something. And at that moment, TD and Sam seemed like the only ones who would help me.

"I guess I am," I said with reluctance. "I guess that's why I'm here."

"Nah, D," T replied. "I *know* that's why you here. And see, it's a lot of fake people out here that might take all your passes and invites and still not have your back when you need it. But that ain't me. You had my back that night at the club and I got yours now. If you want me to I'll get Mirage and break his own gold record over his head."

"It's good to know I got you behind me," I replied earnestly.

"Nah, you got *us*," he said as he began to roll another joint. He reached into the green-filled Ziploc at the foot of the sofa, pulled out enough ganja for five people, and filled two empty blunts, one of which he handed to his brother. "Anything or anybody I got, you got."

I should have felt at ease knowing that I wasn't alone. But instead I saw myself speeding down a dark tunnel toward an unexpected ending. I was trying to breathe water instead of coming up for air. I took a deep hit from T's blunt and listened to what the men before me had to say.

"You don't look like you wanna do this," T prodded just before taking his third puff from the new L. "Before I say anything about what *we* gonna do, you gotta make up your mind that *you* wanna do this. I ain't got nothin' to lose but my parole. I'm *supposed* to get killed in the streets, just like my daddy did. But don't start this if you can't finish it. Don't get us out there and make it be for nothing."

He was giving me a chance to pull out, to save face, to go back to my book deal and my woman and let time do its job of making people forget. I could let it blow over, lay low like Lamar had advised. Mirage wouldn't make a move unless I did.

But Sam and his brother had reminded me of something else. The streets knew what had happened. Everyone in the business knew too. If I didn't make a move, if I moused away from facing him, then I might die feeling like I hadn't represented myself, that I hadn't taken the stand any real man was supposed to.

"So where should we get him at?" I asked decidedly.

"You gotta tell me," he said. "I got the manpower but you gotta let me know how you want to do this. Don't worry about it right now. Just think about it and get back at us."

A pact had been made. And with it I'd been transformed. I'd gone from being an objective observer to a topic of the lyrics and beats that I'd covered for a living. T, Sam, and I slapped hands as I exited the apartment a half hour later. When I reached the street I was still high, but just as scared. If we failed, people could get hurt or even die. But someone had to do this. And if I checked out standing up to Mirage for the greater good

of hip-hop then it would have been worth it. I lit a cigarette and walked east toward the 6 train.

As I navigated the concrete I noted all the differences
between Harlem and Brooklyn. It was a case of pretty
versus dirty, flashy versus shady. Brooklyn had more
parks and brownstones. Harlem had better access to the
city. We both had our strong points. But I was sure that
somewhere in the city's three-hundred-plus-year history
men had foolishly died to prove that their borough was
better than any other. That jabbed at me like words that
hit close to home.

■ ■ ■

"SO WHAT'S GOING on?" Carolina asked from the other
side of our table at Annie's Blue Moon Café. We raised
our voices to be heard above the deafening chatter of
the happy-hour crowd a few feet away at the bar. But it
was the closest place to her office that had decent food.
After dinner she had to go back to her life of mother-
boards and memory chips.

"Nuthin'," I said after too long of a pause. She could
tell that something was wrong. My right hand nervously
tapped against the table, and I was keeping my eyes
away from hers.

"You're not high, are you?" The thought of it, of her man coming to see her under the influence, would have been grounds for an argument, at the very least.

"You know I wouldn't do that," I replied, having actually come down hours before on the train back to Brooklyn. "Just got a lot on my mind."

"Like what?" she asked before taking a forkful of grilled shrimp salad. "You can talk to me about it."

"If I wanted to talk about it I'd be talkin'," I replied. The words were sharper than I'd intended. She gave me a look like she'd just been slapped.

Xiomara was in the past but I still remembered how dangerous it was to have someone who got underneath. My woman was the one person who I should have come clean with. After that remark her narrow eyes begged me to explain myself.

"You didn't have to attack me," she said with a frown.

"I know. I'm sorry. Like I said—"

"I'm just not used to you being this quiet. You usually tell me about your day." Out of the corner of my eye I could see couples at neighboring tables bending their ears in our direction.

"Not today," I said with a sigh. I took a sip from her glass of Merlot, like I always did. I wanted her to touch me in some way. Her hand over mine would have made me feel a million times better.

"Does this have to do with that whole thing in the paper?" Her stockinged toe brushed against my calf under the table. The sensation made me let out a deep exhale.

"Yeah," I said. "It kinda does."

"Don't let him get in your head. Like you said before, it's over and done with."

"Nah it's not, Carolina. I been tryin' to move on but I can't. I gotta do something. I tried once but it didn't work. I gotta do something."

"What do you mean you tried once?" she asked. I had to think of something. And I refused to tell her about the Range Rover.

"I mean I tried—with the article. I called him out in print. And he called me on the phone, told me to watch what I write, said if I didn't he'd kill me." I tried to look calm, but there was nothing calming about the events I'd set in motion.

"He did what?" she asked with salad in her mouth. "What did he do?"

"He called me, said I didn't want to have a war with him. He said that he was gonna put my head in a box. He said he was gon' kill me."

Her hand stretched the width of the table and finally touched mine.

"He's just talking," she said. "Just turn your back, go on with your book and just keep living."

I wished that I could have done what she asked. I

wanted to make her happy but I didn't know if I ever truly could.

"Can I ask you a question?" I proposed. I was looking for an exit, from it all.

"You know the answer," she replied.

"I mean with all the dudes in this city, all the doctors and lawyers, all the niggas with money and nice cribs, why you wit' me?"

"What kind of question is that?" she asked, a furrow of concern in her forehead. "I love you."

"That's not what I'm talking about," I said, desperation in my voice. "What do you see when you look at me? What made you give me your number?"

She paused, still trying to locate the root of my question. In some passive-aggressive way I was trying to make her leave, to steer her clear of what was ahead.

"You know I've dated a lot of men in the five years I've been here," she said, her eyes wandering to the right. "A lot of them had money and gave me things, took me on trips, spoiled me." She stopped to take a sip of water. "But they wanted something for all of that. It was like they wanted to own me, put a collar on me and walk me around the world like a little dog. And something happened, a few months before I met you actually."

"What? Nobody ain't hit you or nothin'?"

"No, but it might've been better if *he* did."

"What happened?"

"He was a lawyer, a very successful one I met at a company party. He was the kind of man my mama would have loved for me. Anyway, we'd been going out for almost six months. And the whole time I was pretty sure that he was seeing someone else, you know, on the side. Don't ask me why, but I was just pretty sure.

"And so I asked him if he was when we were in his car on the way to my house. It was on the way to where he lived in Queens. We had come from this ball and I had on this really nice dress. It was black and the back was out and it hugged my hips the way I like. But anyway we were driving up Lafayette, past Clinton Hill, you know, by the projects. And he told me that if I didn't trust him I could leave. I told him that I didn't want to leave but that I just wanted the truth and he stopped the car. You know what he did?"

"What?"

"He drove me into the parking lot of one of the buildings and pulled me out of the car. He said he didn't need a woman with attitude, who didn't trust him, who didn't know her place. He said I belonged right where I was laying."

My mouth gaped open. I couldn't believe it, couldn't believe that she'd had someone like that in her bed or had been in his. Where had I been? I had to go looking for him next.

"Who is this mutha—"

"Let me finish, D," she said, running a line through my rage. "And so I'm seeing him driving away and I'm thinking to myself that I'm standing in a project parking lot with a twelve-hundred-dollar dress and Prada heels that he bought me. The money didn't mean anything to him. He just threw me away. He could have just lied to me and just said no and I probably would have been perfectly happy.

"But I walked home, about fifteen blocks, in that dress, and those heels. And when I got home I threw both of them in the garbage, right out my window and into the trash thing next to the store. And when I woke up in the morning I told myself that the next man I got with had to be special, someone who really wanted to be with me."

She paused. A smile slowly spread across her face.

"And you're my special man, D. With all your craziness, you're the man I really want to be with."

A warm feeling spun in the center of my chest.

"And I remember the first time I saw you, when you gave me your little lines on the train. I thought you were so cute. But I didn't think that you were special. Then I saw you again, lying there on another train looking like you wanted to cry. The rain was all over you. And the minute I said something you remembered my name. A million women with a million different names in this place and you remembered mine, even though I had *dissed* you. That was special."

"You were special too," I said. There were other words but I couldn't get them out. I wanted to apologize for what was going to come, what might ruin it as a memory.

"Are you okay?" she asked.

"I think so sweetie," I said. I wished that that had been the truth.

■   ■   ■

"YOU EVER COME to a point where it feels like everything's changing but you?" I asked Francine, my bartender, with the thick hairy mole on her right cheek. She was wearing a bad wig that made her look like a cross-dresser. And she was tall enough for the part. But I didn't mind. She always gave me double Hennessy for the single price.

"Plenty of times," she said. Her voice seemed to echo in the emptiness of Frank's Bar. I sipped my drink slowly, thinking about the state of things, and how they would end up.

"And this ain't the last time you gon' feel it either," she added.

I imagined that Frank's was the last vestige of what Fort Greene used to be like, before the buppie and yuppie invasions. I figured it had been the kind of place where blue-collar folks came through for a drink or two before going home to the wife and kids. Francine, with her overdone eye shadow and lipstick, looked like she'd been there long enough to remember that time.

"What you mean?"

"Y'all young folks act like everything is so permanent. But most things in life just go away. You change jobs, change marriages, change houses. It's only a few things that stick with you for the whole time. The world begins and ends a million times before you die."

There wasn't much I could say to that, and as I drained my glass I felt like I needed air, something other than liquor to help me transpose my thoughts. I dropped a ten on the counter and tipped my Braves hat. She nodded at me without another word as I turned to exit.

Outside, the air was warm and humid as I watched scores of cars flashing up and down Fulton Street. The night seemed alive but I had too much on my mind to enjoy it. Action had to be taken. But I needed to know the climate of things first.

Lamar's building was a few blocks away so I decided that a visit was in order. I hadn't talked to him since the day the article came out and I was curious about where my name was on the industry grapevine. So I trudged down to Fort Greene Place and strolled along the tree-lined block, with cars parked in every space, to the corner building that contained his cramped studio. I had to ring the buzzer three times before he answered.

"Who is it!" he yelled through the intercom.

"It's D!" I yelled back with my finger on the talk button.

The electric lock buzzed open and I sprinted up the four narrow flights of stairs to his place, the first one on the left. He opened the door before I could knock.

"So wassup man? What you need?" He had on a greenish satin print robe with the belt tied tightly around his protruding belly. By the tone of his voice I could tell that I'd interrupted something. One of the Smooth Grooves CDs could be heard playing in the background.

"My fault man. You got company?"

"Yeah, you know that intern Cherisse from finance?" He said, speaking loud enough so that Cherisse could easily hear him.

"The one with the real big . . ." I whispered.

"That's right," he said proudly. Her face had been another story. "Got her over here for dinner and now I got the Moët and the slow jams. So you know wassup."

"All right," I said, trying to stop myself from telling him how corny he sounded. "I'll make it quick. Anybody said anything about me since the article came out?"

"Anything about what?"

"About me, about what they think I might do or what Mirage has been sayin'."

He paused to retrieve the data from the rusty filing cabinet in his head.

"Yeah man, people worried about you. You don't go out no more or nuthin' man, like you a fuckin' hermit or somethin'. But speaking of you, did you hear that Mirage and 9–9 are supposed to be havin' some kind of a meetin'?"

"A meetin'? For what? They broke up."

"Well my boy over at Vertigo told me that that's what they meetin' about."

"Where's the meetin'?"

"How the fuck should I know? You don't exactly put out a press release on somethin' like that." He stopped and abruptly craned his head back into the apartment towards his company. I heard a low whisper and knew that Lamar was running out of talking time.

"Well thanks man," I said as I started down the stairwell. "Just be sure to wear dem rubbers."

I didn't expect or wait for his response. Instead I raced back down the stairwell and shoved my face back into the cool night air. I had to figure out where that meeting was going to be. All I had to do was be there with TD and his crew, wait for the meeting to finish, and catch Mirage right after it ended. He'd never see me coming. I'd get him before he got me. I walked towards home reveling in my own brilliance.

But the brilliance I went to sleep with transformed into a series of questions lying on my chest the next morning. Putting my ear to the street would have usually been easy. I was the kind of dude people didn't mind talking to, the kind of cat who you could let things slip to because you knew that he'd protect you. But in the midst of the Mirage thing I might as well have been Bill Clinton. And I was pretty sure that none of my inside contacts wanted to be in the middle of a beef so big that it had turned up in the paper.

There were people I could've asked to help me, like Scott, or Massai Morris. But when you ask journalists for a favor they always have a million questions before they say yes. And once they found out what I was up to they'd more than likely try to stop me. I felt like I'd been checkmated.

Then the phone rang. I knew it was Lamar.

"Yeah," I answered, slightly out of breath from my last set of push-ups.

"You heard, right?" Lamar asked in the giddy voice he used when he had a piping-hot piece of gossip.

"Heard what?"

"You haven't seen the paper?"

"If I had I wouldn't be playing twenty questions wit' your ass," I replied.

"9–9 got arrested last night." If this wasn't bad timing then I didn't know what was.

"For what?"

"Gun possession, hollow-point bullets, and eight ounces of weed."

"Eight ounces? That's enough for intent to distribute. Don't tell me he was that stupid?"

"Gun had the serial number filed off too. Remember when they tried to get Nas on that a few years ago?"

"Yeah. So did he get bail?"

"Nope. They're holdin' 'im. It's all in the *Daily News*, and on all the websites. I just thought I'd give you a heads-up. I guess that Arbor Day meeting's getting rescheduled."

"Yeah," I said, still stunned by the news. "I guess so." My eyes were locked on the kitchen floor. It was pretty dingy and needed a mopping ASAP.

"So what else is up wit' you," he asked.

"Nuthin' really," I said in a spacey voice. "But let me go look at this paper. I'll holla at you later."

"Yup," he replied as he hung up.

I raced to the front door and flung it open to find that my *Daily News* was actually there. I snatched it up and slammed the door behind me. The headline was on the front page: "9–9 Faces 10–10 Years." You had to love those New York tabloid headlines.

Written by none other than Ben Kaufield, the story was pretty extensive in examining the city's case against the other half of Arbor Day.

Arthur Ballard, a.k.a. 9–9, chose the wrong night for speeding on Fordham Road in the Bronx. After pulling him over, officers Lamar Maddox and Steven Gaffney found more than 8 ounces of marijuana underneath the driver's seat of his 1998 BMW 850i and an unregistered firearm loaded with hollow-point bullets in the glove compartment.

"These charges are ridiculous," said Randall Brown, Ballard's attorney. "My client is the victim of the same kind of Bronx police corruption that has brought about the deaths and wrongful imprisonment of too many young men of color in this City." Brown, however, had no comment on the seemingly open-and-shut nature of the case.

According to District Attorney Allen Woods, police had been investigating Ballard for some time, after they received an anonymous tip that the rapper/actor was selling guns and drugs out of the three locations of his 9 Lives chain of record stores in the Bronx and Queens. An arraignment hearing is scheduled for next week. Ballard is expected to be released on bail later in the day.

I had the urge to throw the paper down and step on it. Something didn't seem right. The arrest seemed a little too convenient. And I knew that anyone who was really moving that kind of weight would have been a lot more careful. But I couldn't let Arthur Ballard's legal troubles consume me. I was after Mirage.

■ ■ ■

"SO HAVE YOU given any thought about the cover?" Todd asked me in his cubbyhole of an office on 50th Street, just off of Lexington.

I was only there in body, still trying to think of how I could find Mirage and orchestrate the attack. But I didn't have a single idea.

"I was thinking about having this dude, you know in like khakis and a T-shirt, pointing two nine-millimeters straight ahead, like he's aimin' them at the viewer." I stood up and mimicked the pose with imaginary weapons.

"Well, people would definitely get the point, huh?" he said with a facetious grin.

"Yeah, they definitely would," thinking that he was actually taking the idea seriously.

"Well, how about something a little more subtle," he said, knowing that a cover like that wasn't going to be chosen at a high-gloss publishing house like Pressman.

"Nah, not really," I replied. "That was my only one."

His desk, which seemed a little high for him, was in full disarray. Post-it notes, pens, and red pencils seemed to be everywhere. Manuscripts were stacked high on the left corner of his desk, and behind him was a small shelf, lined with empty bottles of imported beers. The only ones I recognized were Heineken and Corona. And the latest edition of the *Village Voice* was spread out in front of him, only inches beneath his chin as he slouched over.

"Well, I'm sure that the art department will come up with something," he replied.

"Yeah," I said. But something caught my eye in the *Voice* he had, even though I was reading it upside down.

"Can I see that?" I asked, pointing to the paper.

He picked it up like a fragile thing and handed it to me with it still open to the same page. The ad jumped out at me immediately. Mirage had a show on Friday night. It was Thursday.

The eighth-of-a-page ad proclaimed that S.O.B.'s was presenting Mirage, from Arbor Day, on Friday, April 24, 1999, at 11 p.m. There was a special note that he'd be previewing his new album along with a few Arbor Day classics. Todd said something while I was reading but I didn't even catch it.

"What?" I asked, hoping that he'd repeat it.

"I asked you if you were all right. You look weird. By the way, how's the arm?"

"Good as new," I said, still sounding distracted.

"I heard about—"

"It wasn't as serious as they made it out to be," I replied, heading him off at the pass. Chad had given me similar condolences via a phone call weeks earlier, just after I'd gotten out of the hospital.

"I read the paper the other day. I saw what you said in that article. You were just being figurative, right?"

I gave him a blank expression that slowly turned into a smile.

"I guess you'll figure out soon," I said.

The fake laughs we belted out didn't come close to convincing each other that I had been joking.

"Call me if you need anything else," I said, as I grabbed my jacket and headed out of his office.

"Sure," he said behind me. "And stay out of trouble." I didn't say anything else before I closed his office door behind me.

■ ■ ■

"YO T?" I yelled into the payphone, wishing that I had given in to the current cell craze.

"So what the deal?" he asked, getting straight to the point.

"He got a show Friday night at S.O.B.'s. Start at eleven."

"Then we'll put a plan together. Come by the house at nine or so."

"You got it," I said, as if it was all a routine exercise.

As soon as I dropped the receiver in its cradle, I was overwhelmed with a familiar sinking feeling. The clock was about to strike twelve. And soon my manufactured past would come down like the Berlin Wall. In conversations I'd told TD, Sam, and a million others that back at home I'd delivered beatdowns, that I'd dodged bullets, that I was a man from the mean streets of the Dirty South.

And it wasn't totally a lie. I *was* from the 'hood, and I'd seen and heard a lot. Growing up on the raunchiest part of Fair Street, my boys James, the twins Ricky and Mikey, BJ and Monty had enjoyed a good share of neighborhood warfare. I just hadn't been with them for most of it. I was usually trapped inside doing my homework and keeping to my mama's curfew. But I had been there for a few things. Well, one thing.

It was the year of tenth grade, I was with them when they'd caught two dudes from Hope Homes projects who'd tried to rape James's sister. James and BJ had grabbed them while they were trying to climb over the back fence to the parking lot.

James started it and the twins joined in behind him. Then BJ and Monty added a few kicks and punches. I felt every blow they delivered from the sidelines, imagining what it must have felt like for the two on the ground, boy-men who were blocks away from anyone who could help them. But they deserved it.

They had committed the worst crime. And they were being punished in the only way we knew. But no matter how much we rained down on them, we couldn't do anything about the fact that Loretta, the victim, wouldn't touch or even go out with another man outside her family for almost three years. It seemed like it was even a struggle for her to wave to us whenever we came past her window.

I stood there and watched as the beating commenced. Watching and remembering was my special skill. James was eyeing the metal baseball bat between my hands as if it were a priceless jewel. I always carried it because I was the youngest and the smallest. That would have made me the prime target when I was alone and out of bounds. But I never went out of bounds. The bat was just for show.

But that weapon became serious business when James pried it from my hands. I had a bad feeling about what was going to happen. I just knew that two souls were about to leave their bodies and travel downward towards hell. They already looked lifeless as they laid there in the fetal position, muttering to each other in anguish.

I made out one's cries for help, his tears mixing with the blood on his face. James examined the bat closely, stamping it with his seal of approval. Then he handed it back to me. It was my turn.

At the time I hadn't hit anyone since the fifth grade. But I was Fair Street. That was supposed to supersede everything. So I found a gallon of courage, raised the bat, and started swinging downwards repeatedly. I heard a bone crack, imagining the blisters and bruises I was inflicting.

More blood splattered across summer short-sleeved shirts and shorts. The Hotlanta heat pulled sweat from my pores in streams and at the end I wondered if I had delivered the fatal blows. But I could hear their shallow breathing as if their mouths were right next to my ears. We left them there. Someone called an ambulance and they were saved.

Four weeks later someone shot James in the Sojourner Truth College parking lot, right after he dropped off his girl, who went to school there. A war started between us and Hope that lasted for the rest of high school. James had never seen it coming. He'd done something for the right reason but hadn't expected it to come back to him, not like that.

I was trembling again at the corner of 51st and Park, still standing by the payphone, unnoticed music still pouring out of the stereo headphones around my neck. I hadn't thought about that day in a long time. In a crew every-one covers each other's back. In this case TD and Sam were covering mine and together we were fighting for something, for my life, and for the way our game was supposed to be played.

DAKOTA GRAND

But if it was that concrete then why was I scared? It had to be taken care of, this Mirage thing, so the calls and the dreams and scars would go away. There wasn't another option. I told myself that playing the spectator in this exchange could have gotten me dead. My nerves slowly found composure and I hopped a 4 train back to Brooklyn.

■ ■ ■

TWO MESSAGES WERE waiting when I got up the next morning. The first was from Carolina, who was worried about me since she hadn't heard from me in a day and a half. But the second was from Scott. He was finally back in town and he wanted me to meet him for lunch, at a place called Iguana on West 54th and Eighth Avenue, in an area on the West Side that I wasn't too familiar with.

"At least you don't still look like a nigga who got his ass kicked," Scott said facetiously.

"I guess you heard about it then," I said somewhat shamefully.

His suit was jet black and he wore a dark blue shirt and matching tie. His beard was freshly trimmed and he had new glasses, brown tortoiseshell Ralph Lauren frames. If I wore glasses I would have wanted a pair like his. I ordered Hennessy straight up while he had a scotch and soda.

"Like I don't read the paper?" he replied. "But I should've heard it from *you.*"

"Was I supposed to call and tell you how I got my ass beat?"

"You should've let me know," he said with concern.

"What, you was gonna go beat him up for me?" I said semi-sarcastically, blindly hoping that he might have given me a yes.

"*No*, but I coulda got you a good lawyer," he replied.

Just then the waiter returned and we both ordered. I had the chicken quesadilla and a salad. Scott decided on the sizzling fajita platter.

"Nah, I'm not gonna handle it that way," I said after I chased a sip of my drink with some water. "I ain't takin' him to court."

I scanned the level where we were sitting. The walls were covered in dark wainscotting. The silver taps on the bar were polished to a gleaming shine. I was the only person in the place who didn't have a tie on.

"What do you mean?" Scott barked. "How are you going to handle it?"

"Somebody's gotta take a stand, man, show 'em that we ain't gettin' beat down every time they don't like what we write."

"Oh, so that's what that quote in the paper meant. You're a crimefighter now? Dakota Grand isn't a bad name for a superhero. But you gotta have a sidekick—"

"This ain't a joke," I replied, trying to deepen my voice for emphasis. "It ain't right, Scott. It ain't right. He almost killed me."

"He broke your arm and cracked some ribs, gave you a concussion. Yeah, he worked your ass over. But you weren't gonna die."

"Man, he played me out in front of the whole industry, like I was some kind of a hoe! People in the street know about it!" Heads turned our way at the tables closest to us. My voice was carrying. Scott held his comments until after our slim-faced, long-nosed waiter had refilled our water glasses.

"So what are you going to do? Ambush him while he's onstage at some club? Catch an assault charge, be the first hip-hop writer to hit the front page in a scandal?"

"You know I wouldn't go out like that. Dakota Grand wouldn't get caught."

"That won't be what they call you in jail, in the hospital, or anywhere else. And wassup with referring to yourself in the third person?"

"You know, I would've figured my friend might have more faith in me," I said, treating him like my words and actions weren't completely ridiculous.

"When it comes to words on a page, yeah. But I'm listenin' to you now and it sounds like some sick joke. You a writer, D. Dukin' it out in the street doesn't go with the job description. And I hate to tell you this, but Mirage won't be the only person who ever threatens you or tries to hurt you."

"You ever got beat down like I did?" I asked.

"No," he said plainly.

"Then how the hell do you know what it's like to get stomped on by three niggas just 'cuz you told the truth? He said he was gonna send my head home in a box."

"People *say* a lot of things," he replied. "What they do is another story. You worry about dying when he's got a gun to your head, when you see him through the peephole banging on your door, when you know that the threat is real."

"We can't have them doing this to us," I said, ignoring his point. I would have done anything for him to tell me that I was right. "I can't be looking out for these people, trying to protect them in print, when they put me in the hospital."

"You got it right there. Don't protect them then. But keep in mind, the artists are not your enemies. You're talking about one boy with extreme delusions of grandeur. Getting physical won't solve the problem. No matter what you do, things like this are gonna keep goin' on. They always have, and whenever they do somebody's number comes up to take the fall. That time it was yours. Don't make a big thing out of it."

His words circled my head like a satellite. It didn't

take long to admit that he was probably right. There it was, Friday, and in less than eight hours I'd have been making my move. But I'd finally been made to see the light. Attacking Mirage wouldn't change anything. And even if he did, some other artist would do it to someone else, just because he or she could.

"I don't like to take losses, Scott," I replied with a defeated sigh.

"Get used to it," he said plainly. "Like they say, sometimes it's not until you really lose that you're fully able to win. Besides, you'll get the last laugh. They'll never last as long as you."

He was right. Living under the shadow of corporate control it was usually two albums and you were out of there. I'd seen the demise of more music careers than I could count. I'd had the Shroud serve me a drink, only a few years after having a major hit. I would be the one to win just by walking away, just by living my life.

■ ■ ■

SHE HAD GONE home from work early. I couldn't explain it but I knew that she had. I also knew she was in her bedroom, sleeping on the cramped mattress she always argued was good for her back. And I knew her uncle was still downstairs working in the store and chain-smoking his pipe like a Cuban Sherlock Holmes. Knowing all of those things I knocked on her front door.

She answered almost immediately in my Sojourner Truth sweatpants and a tank top, her nipples perking through its thin material.

"What are you doing here?" she asked groggily, as if she'd just gotten up. She smiled.

I smiled back but didn't say anything. Then I kissed her, our tongues eventually wandering between each other's teeth.

"I missed you," she said.

"I know," I said. I took her hand and we went into the bedroom, where I carefully laid her down and slowly lifted the tank top over her head. I gently bit and sucked both nipples, my free hand crawling between her thighs. The sounds she made helped me to quickly rise to the occasion. Soon after, I entered and we became one. We climaxed, and then dropped deep into our respective dreams.

■ ■ ■

"WHAT'S WRONG?" SHE asked me as we sat on a bench on Eastern Parkway watching the sunset. Half of the orange globe was already beneath the row of brownstones in front of us.

"What do you mean?"

"I haven't seen or heard from you in a day and a half. And what was with you at lunch the other day?"

"I've just been busy, sweetie. That's why I came by."

"It's more than busy," she said. "You weren't . . . yourself."

"Look, I'm sorry about all that but you know I been thinking and well—"

"What is it, D?"

"Well—" I paused again.

"What is it?"

"Let's go to Cuba," I blurted. "And I want to go soon. I'll pay for it. I got some of that advance money left over." For some reason I was fighting to get the words out. "I just need to get out of here and—"

She put a finger to my lips and kissed me on the cheek. "Okay," she said plainly.

"Really? Well when—"

"Whenever you want," she replied. She was too calm about it. That made me nervous.

"What are you gonna do about work? You can't just up and leave."

"You let me worry about work."

"That's it?" I asked.

"That's it," she said as she leaned in for me to put my arm around her. She smiled to herself as she watched the sun continue its descent.

"Okay then," I said. "There's one more thing I need from you."

"What?"

"Come over tonight. I just want you with me."

"Sure," she said. "I want to be with you too."

■ ■ ■

DARKNESS SWALLOWED THE remaining sunlight and a cab made a short trip from Crown Heights to Clinton Hill. I was glad that it was over, that I hadn't dragged her into my short-lived madness. She went back into the bedroom just after seven and was in a deep snoring sleep five minutes later.

But I wasn't tired. And as I sat there flipping through channels I needed something to do. I looked down at the coffee table and saw that the new *Maintain* had arrived. I usually just pitched the new issues, still in plastic, into the towering piles of magazines in the corner. But Lamar had told me to crack it open this time. He'd said that he had a surprise for me.

I clawed away the plastic and began to flip through the pages. I ignored the table of contents and decided to just skim through the images and text to see if I could find what he was talking about. It didn't take me long.

Lamar's piece on Mirage was a full three-columned

with a photo of the two of them talking, head to
head, in the *Maintain* conference room. It had been taken
just before he beat me down in the lobby. I knew it because he had the same clothes on.

Entitled "Was It Real? Or Just a Mirage?" the piece
started out in the usual Lamar fashion, with allusions to
the man's greatness followed by commentary on how
Arbor Day was the most underrated group in hip-hop
history. But just when I'd had enough of the flattery, he
surprised me. He dove into the issues.

> "Everything [Grand] said was an absolute lie," Mirage
> says. "I don't share the details of my personal life with
> the public. I don't like when these reporters want to
> come out and lie on me. I'm definitely gonna see him
> in court." But despite his claims, *Maintain* received a
> copy of Mr. Grand's original interview tape only to
> find that not once was the rapper misquoted. On the
> tape Mirage even goes into more descriptive detail
> than what Mr. Grand's article presents.

And it got worse as it went along. Lamar had dug up a
few former Arbor Day associates to corroborate the
early stages of Mirage's breakdown. One source referred
to a violent argument at a birthday party where Mirage
apparently mashed a piece of cake into his wife's face.
Another spoke of his paranoia, of him slapping his for-

mer manager, Polyné Wilson, and Wilson's almost immediate decision to drop him from his management roster. He'd found things that I hadn't, gotten quotes from people even I couldn't reach. He'd exposed Mirage again, just in case there was any doubt about the piece I'd written. And I knew that he'd done it for me, that he'd done it just to prove that I was right, to let me know that I hadn't been put in the hospital for nothing.

Nothing could have made me smile more as I finished the last paragraph. I had to call him to express my thanks and to give him my congratulations on the best piece that he'd ever written. There was another real journalist in a house full of fakers. I was about to buy Lamar as many drinks as I could afford. But the phone rang before I could pick it up.

"D!" Lamar yelled into the receiver.

"Hey man, what—"

"Yo man you gotta fuckin' help me!"

"What?"

"It's two dudes tryin' to break into my house!" I could hear what sounded like a hammer hitting his door in the background.

It snapped into my head like a piece in an almost finished puzzle. I knew who they were the minute he said it. I'd met them in the lobby of the *Maintain* building. Mirage had gotten smarter. He'd sent others to do his dirty work while he was on his way to a show.

"Did you call the cops?"

"Yeah, man. But get over here man! Now!" I heard a louder thud and the line clicked off.

There was a brief moment when I stood there, in nothing but boxers and socks, wondering how it had all spun this far out of control. Mirage had started out being my ticket to the big time and now I felt like the unlikely hero in some B-rated suspense thriller. I grabbed my pants and shirt off the floor and got dressed quickly. I didn't even call to tell Carolina that I was leaving.

The distance between my apartment and Lamar's was about twelve blocks. I Michael Johnsoned down Clinton to DeKalb Avenue and then sped down the hill like my friend's life depended on it. Maybe it did. I was shedding sweat in buckets as my mind began to ask me what the hell I was going to do against two men without any kind of a weapon. What if they had guns? What if Lamar was dead by the time I got there?

My muscles started to burn as I passed Tillie's Café. My feet felt like they were running barefoot on the warm concrete beneath them. I almost flattened a middle-aged woman with a dog and some groceries, but did a Jamal Anderson juke and avoided her. I heard the echo of a car collision on the other side of the park. Fort Greene Place came into view. I could see the flashing lights before I turned the corner. I thought I was too late.

But Lamar was sitting on the stoop of his building, his

head in his hands but seemingly untouched. I slowed to a walking pace as I saw two cops standing on the steps before him. I didn't have to look twice to see that it was Roberts and Meadows with their guns holstered, pens moving swiftly over little pads. Lamar looked up and saw me approaching.

"It's all right, man!" he yelled. "They scared 'em off. Put a big dent in my door though."

The officers spun around and saw me there, dripping with perspiration, the buttons on my shirt through the wrong holes. I'd wanted to be the one that made the rescue.

"Six degrees, huh?" Roberts said with a sarcastic grin.

"Yeah," I replied, as I shifted my attention to Lamar. "What happened?"

"I was just tellin' them. I don't know how they got in the front door. They musta waited for somebody to come in or somethin'. But they started banging on the door, sayin' that they was gonna kill me if I didn't open up."

"You see their faces?" I asked.

"Why don't you let us ask the questions," Meadows barked. There appeared to be a stain of some sort on his uniform, probably coffee and doughnut powder.

"Sorry," I said.

"But anyway," Lamar went on as if the boys in blue weren't there, "I ducked down and kept the chain on and called 911. Then I called you. But nah, I didn't see their face. They had stockins over 'em so I couldn't see what they looked like. One of 'em had dreads though."

"Do you have any idea of who they could've been?" Roberts asked.

"Made any enemies recently?" Meadows followed up.

"Hey, I'm just a magazine editor, man. I ain't got no enemies." The two officers looked at each other and then glanced over at me.

"Well, we'll go up and take a look in the hallway, see if they left anything behind that we can use," Roberts said. Lamar nodded and the men entered through the open front entranceway, leaving the two of us alone.

"I read the article," I said, still out of breath. "You know—"

"Yeah, I know," he replied with a grin. "I had to do somethin'. I wasn't going to let you go out like that without doing my little part to get you some payback."

"I don't know if it was worth it, though," I said.

"That muthafucka's career is over anyway," he said, trying to act like he hadn't been scared out of his mind until the cops came. "Sometimes you gotta stand up."

Lamar was the least likely person to say something like that. He looked both ways and behind him in his own house. But yet and still he had seen where I was coming from. He knew that there was a rabid dog at

S.O.B.'s that needed to be put down. I looked down and saw that he was clutching his cell phone tightly in his right hand. What made sense didn't matter anymore.

"Can I see your phone?" He handed it to me without a word and I checked the time. It was eight-thirty. I dialed a number. It only rang once before TD picked up.

"I'm a little late. But I'm on my way."

"We got you," he said, just before he hung up. I hit the end button and gave my friend his phone back.

"You goin' to the Mirage show?"

"At S.O.B.'s? Yeah, right. After this I might be goin' out of town for a while."

"No need to do that," I said calmly. "This'll all be over within a minute."

"Huh?" he asked, a look of concern on his face.

"I'm about to finish this." I could hear Roberts and Meadows on their way back out. "I'll holler at you later." And with that, I disappeared into the Brooklyn night like a caped crusader.

■ ■ ■

"AND IT'S THE muthafuckin' man of the hour!" TD yelled as he welcomed me into his closet of an apartment.

He was dressed more like a presenter at the Grammys

than a Harlem hard rock. The pattern on his shiny silk shirt appeared to be a bowl of fruit on a gold-and-white-striped background. White pants and shoes completed the ensemble.

"So you ready?" he asked as if we were heading out strictly to party.

"You know it," I said in my best tough-guy tone. Sam emerged from the bathroom in a pair of khakis and a golf shirt, his clothing a little closer to suiting the occasion.

"So where's everybody else?" I asked.

"Downstairs," TD said. "We'll head down there to get 'em in a quick minute, put a plan together. But first we gotta finish this L."

He had already rolled and lit. The rotation, from Sam to myself and back to him, began soon after. One of my rules about getting high was that I didn't do it when I had something important to do. But that night I needed it. With the nature of the task ahead, both slight paranoia and irrational impulse became more assets than drawbacks. I took in deep pulls, trying to inhale the courage I needed to complete the upcoming task.

"So how you wanna do this?" Sam asked me, as if we were planning a jewel heist. I'd had plenty of time to strategize on the train ride up.

"It's real simple. We walk in the front door like everybody else, move to the front, and as soon as he comes out we rush the stage. Y'all follow after me and we stomp that nigga into wine."

"Stomp him into wine?" Sam laughed. "What the fuck does that mean?"

"I guess that's some Down South shit," I said.

"Yeah, that sounds like some country-ass bullshit y'all would say Down South," TD replied. "I should know since I used to be down there when I was in college."

"You was in school? What school?" The image of TD carrying books on a campus just didn't seem believable.

"Alabama A&M. I was up there for about a year, back when I first started tryin' to go legit. But it wasn't for me so I left."

"You don't seem like the type to want to go to college," I said.

"What, because I don't speak pro-per English?" he said giggling, the high kicking in. We all began to laugh uncontrollably, like cartoon villains pleased with a perfect plan destined to go awry. But it did feel good to laugh.

"But hey, what about security in the club?" Sam asked.

"Oh yeah," I said as the weed began to have its effect. "Take the biggest dudes we got and use 'em to block 'em. How many we got includin' us?"

"Six."

"That's enough," I said. "It ain't gonna take six people

to beat him down. And I'm sayin' . . . I'm tryin' to beat this nigga as close to death as I can without killin' him."

"I hear you on that," TD said. I liked the feeling I was getting, from the weed and my own twisted mind. I felt like I could stop bullets, like nothing Mirage did could hurt me. I was smarter this time, and when the night was over, he was going to remember the name Dakota Grand for the rest of his life.

After a half hour Sam corralled us downstairs to another apartment, where the rest of my supposed army was waiting. He banged on the door twice and it swung open instantly. A man wider than the doorframe and seemingly older than all of us answered with a worried expression on his face.

"Oh it's y'all," he said. His face eased into a smile. "Thought you was the landlord. Ain't paid the rent for this month, son." The fat man took a few steps back and we entered by walking past him.

The place was wider than TD's but still relatively small. Inside there were four others: two skinny boys who wouldn't have looked eighteen with beards, a stocky dude with dreads, and an Indian-looking guy about our age who seemed higher than us. This was what I had to work with.

"This is your crew?" I asked.

"Hey man, these *men* be about their business," TD replied with an emphasis on the m-word.

"Man, I'm not tryin' to go in here and get my ass whipped again," I said. The high had me speaking loudly, potentially insulting the people who were there to back me up. Fortunately, they were too high to really notice.

"Why not? You did it before," Sam said, laughing. His brother exploded into laughter behind him and everyone else joined in. The thought of knocking a few of little brother's teeth out came to mind and then got lost in the haze.

"Whatever," I said.

Fat boy was soon introduced as Ali. I learned that he worked for the post office. He was very fat and moved very slowly. But I had no doubt that he could hold off a security guard or two long enough for us to do our thing. The two skinny boys were Trinidadian, cousins named Trevor and Dennis. The dreaded muscle man was Dave, an ex-bouncer who had been blacklisted from the club game for always getting high on the job. He looked like another good blocker. And the Indian-looking fellow was Ralph, the one I learned absolutely nothing about for the whole three hours I spent with him. TD had told them all to wear boots, the steel-toed kind that were good for stomping. I'd worn my heavy Timberland boots, with the leather around the ankle, just for the occasion.

"All right y'all," I said like a coach in the locker room

before kickoff. "This is the deal. We gon' go in like everybody else, get our drink on, whatever. But when Mirage come out on that stage, everybody has a job to do." The small mob mumbled and nodded in the affirmative.

"Ali and Ralph, y'all gotta block off security. When we come in, see where they is in the club and get close to 'em. The rest of us is gonna rush the stage. You gotta keep 'em from gettin' to us."

"No problem," Dave said just before he took his last pull on a roach. Ali nodded but I could tell that he was a little unsure of himself.

"For the rest of y'all it's real easy. When we come in, space yourself out. We can't let him know what we there for. He might see me, but don't worry about that. 'Cuz I'm gonna be the first one to hit him."

"You sure you—" TD tried to interject.

"I'll be the first one to hit 'em," I reiterated. "I'm the one with the score to settle. But once y'all start don't stop hittin' 'im until I stop. When we're done we jet out the side exit and that's it." Everyone nodded in agreement again and we were off.

I felt like I was in total control when we stumbled out of Ali's apartment a few minutes later. I felt the adrenaline rush through me like scalding water as we inched closer to the 1 train.

It was a long ride down on the local line but it gave us

a chance for our respective highs to thin. It was too simple of a plan for them to have any questions. The closer we got the more they seemed ready. It was an added treat that like TD, most of them hated Mirage's music.

Both my heart and mind were racing uncontrollably as the club finally came into view. I lit a cigarette and told myself that it would be my last. After it was finished I could quit smoking and not have to sneak out to the stoop in the middle of the night for a square whenever Carolina was over. And with that thought I remembered that she would be still at my place, probably sleeping, unaware that her man was off on a high-risk maneuver. I believed that I would walk out of that club as the winner. But I couldn't be sure. I had to let her know.

"I'll be right back!" I said to my men as I cut across the street to the payphone and inserted a quarter. I called her voice mail, which she sometimes checked in the middle of the night. Her recorded message somehow managed to relax me a little. But when I heard the beep I once again became a man with a job to do.

"Baby it's me. I'm sorry I ran out and didn't tell you where I was going. But this Mirage thing has gotten out of hand. He went after Lamar for an article he wrote too. And I can't stand for it no more. I'm about to go after him. I'm about to let him know that he can't run around doin' this to us, that he isn't gonna make me afraid in my own damn city. But just in case I don't make it back, just in case somethin' happens, I just want you to know that I love you, and that there's no one else that I would have rather spent the rest of my life with. Thank you for giving me a chance. And hopefully I'll see you soon."

When the whole thing had started months before, everything in my world had been so plastic and so repetitive. I'd wanted to write for the big boys and live the good life. I'd wanted to do something important. But on the verge of the most important thing I'd done in my three years in the city, I once again wondered if what I was doing was really worth it. But then I thought about Lamar, about Fields, about WWII, about me laying on the marble floor in a lobby broken in pieces for doing what was right. And I felt like this was the only way to get even.

"What was up with the phone call?" Trevor asked.

"Insurance," I said coldly as we filtered into the club.

The line outside of S.O.B.'s stretched the length of the block. All of the faces looked familiar. As I approached the front I saw Massai Morris pleading with the clipboard girl before he headed towards the back of the line in defeat. Unfortunately, he seemed to be learning things the hard way.

I knew the curvy Asian girl at the front holding the list from somewhere. But I didn't know where. Luckily she did. She'd been one of the interns at MCA back when I did artist bios for them. She called me over, gave me a light kiss on the cheek, and let all of us jump the line. I tried to signal Morris to follow us in but he seemed to think that I was just waving at him.

Two bouncers gave us full pat-downs before we slid inside. The DJ was in the midst of his reggae set and as planned the group splintered off into various parts of the relatively small space.

As I moved through the crowd I scanned all the generic faces and pointing fingers, people whispering to their respective cliques that I, Dakota Grand, had resurfaced in the cesspool. They wore their designer labels proudly as they ran their mouths about gossip and sales figures, exchanging their elaborate business cards with every hug and handshake. But the attention they gave me didn't last too long. After I passed there would be someone else to look at, another topic for their idle chatter.

I looked at the world I used to be a part of, people holding overpriced drinks in tiny, dim little spaces. That life was the habit that I'd been trying to kick when Mirage and I had first sat down a season before. And even with *The Magazine* and *Caution* and everything else I'd gone on to do, I was there again, even if this time I did have a mission to accomplish.

"Make it fast," I said to the effeminate bartender. I ordered a brew for a change, a Corona, and he quickly obliged. Then I studied my warped reflection in the mirror, again. The scars had all vanished, as had the marks on my ribs and the strange sensitivity on the skin over my recently mended humerus. I looked like myself again. Another index finger jabbed my shoulder.

I swung around again figuring that it was some all too familiar person who I'd chatted with a million times too many. But instead I was greeted by someone who I'd never actually met.

Tyrone Fields was shorter than I'd figured, but otherwise matched the photos I'd seen of him. While I wasn't the biggest fan of his column in *Manhole* I had to give it up to him for being a veteran of the game. Thirty-five was old for what we did. The graying hairs around the edges of his hairline proved it.

"Dakota Grand," he said, grinning. "You know I've been wanting to meet you for a while."

"For real? What you wanna meet me for?"

"Because you're my hero," he replied. I laughed unexpectedly.

"You got a good sense of humor, man," I replied.

"Nah, I'm serious," he yelled over the increasingly loud beats behind us. "You stood up for us in that article, man. I said my piece. But you went all out and said what some of us shoulda said back in the day. Maybe it's about time one of these artists gets his ass beat to see how it feels." He was leaning against the bar and his speech was slurred.

"They gonna know how it *feels*," I said as if I was joking. "I promise." Soon after he offered a sloppy handshake and dissolved into the thickening crowd.

I looked around the room to see if my team was still in position. They were. Most were swigging on brews or trying to talk to the T&A contingent. But they were where they were supposed to be. TD's eyes met mine and we nodded to each other in recognition. I made my way to the front.

On my way through the sizable crowd, Field's words kept a grin on my grille. Even he, the king of nice guy reviews, knew that this menace had to be stopped. I was doing it for me. I was doing it for Lamar. And I was doing it for him too. It was unanimous. I, Dakota Grand, the twenty-two-year-old out-of-town kid from Southwest Atlanta, was right, and ready.

The house DJ faded out and the show's host came in. A clown from one of the local radio stations, he emerged backed by three interns who were throwing promotional T-shirts into the crowd. He made jokes about the heat in the club and how "a group of blacks and latinos stuck in a room together" could put the power company out of business. The crowd laughed but

I didn't. I held my position, playfully twirling my now empty Corona bottle in my right hand.

The host's shtick went on for another ten minutes while Mirage's DJ, Rain Man, set up for the show. I wondered if Mirage himself had even arrived yet. He had no idea how memorable the night was going to be for the both of us.

"Give it up for Mirage!" the clown yelled as he exited the stage through the side door.

Rain Man started the show by a cut into "Trees No Seeds," Arbor Day's most successful anthem. The crowd came alive as Mirage emerged in the midst of the frenzy wearing a red Ecko hoodie, baggy jeans, and boots. He'd shaved his head bald and he looked surprisingly happy.

My body moved uncontrollably to songs that had been branded into my brain after years of listening. I'd purchased two copies of everything they'd ever put out just in case one got damaged. I'd made a tape of all the videos and had even made a date out of showing them to Carolina, in the order in which they were released. That night was actually the first I'd seen him perform since I'd come to New York.

I even mouthed the chorus, moving closer to him to further immerse myself in the sound. But it didn't tear me away from my focus. Rain Man brought in the beat for "Smoke and Mirrors." I was almost to the front.

Toes were stepped on and drinks were spilled. Boyfriends called after me and their females spat curses to my back. But I wasn't concerned with them. When I stopped I was standing right under his nose. Our eyes met, just before he recited the first line. I had him.

"You!" he yelled right into the mic, giving me a déjà vu feeling I couldn't place. There we were, two men somewhat face to face, what I'd said I wanted all along. That same leg began to tremble.

He seemed bigger than I'd remembered, massive. He leapt off the stage and I staggered backward just in time to get clear of him. The mic was still in his hand.

"What the fuck are you doin' here?" he asked with a grin, as if he really had me cornered. The crowd probably thought that it was part of the show. If I'd had a gun I don't even think I could have pulled the trigger. But he apparently had something else to say, something he didn't want the rest of the club to hear.

He lowered the mic as he took another step toward me. In doing so he'd left his head wide open to attack. He said I couldn't beat him, that I couldn't even try. I wasn't going to give him the chance to say or do anything else.

I gripped the bottle in my hand and swung my right arm in a perfect arc. The bottle disintegrated against the side of his skull and a stream of blood began to flow from the wound. The mic hit the floor with a booming thud that made the walls vibrate. Rain Man hadn't stopped the music. I was far from being done.

He was still standing, staring at me in disbelief, blood beginning to trickle down his face. I struck him across the jaw with a left and a right, then two lefts, and another right. He fell backwards and almost hit his head on the edge of the stage. I stepped forward and jammed my boot into his chest. He let out a high-pitched chok- ing sound. I heard screaming and yelling all behind me, the sounds of the crowd running for cover and the exits. I turned to look for my army. They were coming. Dave and Ali wrestled with two huge bouncers while Sam and the rest were fighting their way through the fleeing crowd. I turned back around. I couldn't have been turned around for more than a second. But when our eyes met again Mirage was reaching under his shirt. I stepped in to kick him again but saw a flash of something metal. I raised my foot. He pulled the trigger.

The first bullet screamed upward through my thigh. The projectile burned like a white-hot needle. The sec- ond one knocked me backwards with the force of a two- ton medicine ball and the third screamed past my right ear and I started falling. On the way to the floor I saw TD jump into the line of fire. Then I heard two more shots as the back of my head smacked against the floor. TD hit the ground right after me, holding his hand and rolling around screaming in pain. That was when the rest of the crew finally rushed in past us. Sam came first, then Trevor, then the others. I could hear fists and heels beating heavily against my enemy. He didn't get a chance to fire another shot.

We were all laying there, Mirage, TD, and I. Aside from the sounds of pummeling, the room seemed silent as the sizzling lights above shone hotly down on us. Mirage let out a terrible scream just as my limbs began to twitch violently. I couldn't see anything except for the ceiling, but my ears were wide open. I'd never expected to be missing all the action, again. Then there was a loud explosion behind me, followed by the pattering of hard-soled shoes and the cocking of standard-issue Beretta 9mms.

I waited for the forty-one shots but they never came. There were so many questions that they seemed to be coming out of my pores. Would they call the paramedics or would they leave us all to bleed to death on the linoleum-tiled dance floor? There was the sound of more bodies hitting the deck. My mind wandered away from the scene. Had Carolina gotten my message yet? Would I live to see *Caution* go into print?

Time danced in different directions. The lights above me seemed to go dim. I could feel the blood leaving me, the very liquid ashamed that it had played a part in the mess of it all. I didn't think I was going to make it.

I saw flashing red and white lights, people in uniforms

with both guns and medical equipment. I saw red flares and police blockades. And I remembered seeing Fields's face behind a barrier that looked so far away from me. All of my fears went away, all of the needs for anything, except for her. And the good thing about it was that I was still alive.

■ ■ ■

"I COULD CARE less about you," District Attorney Joshua Grayer said. He stood in front of my hospital bed, two Roberts-and-Meadows-like cops right behind him. My right wrist was cuffed to my bed, as if I was going to get far with two bullet wounds and no crutches. "I just want Michael Adkins."

I knew that I didn't have a lot of bargaining chips. They had me on assault and disturbing the peace. TD was facing a possible parole violation, and the rest of the gang, the ones who had actually been caught, had been slapped with charges as well. As I said before, I didn't like cops. But vigilantism thus far had proved to be very hazardous to my health.

"I'm willing to let everybody walk away from this if you testify against Adkins. Identify him as the man who attacked you, and as the same one who shot you last night."

The *New York Post* was in my lap, the headline screaming: "Writer and Rapper Go Head to Head in Club Battle." It was the kind of headline I expected, sensational and vague, words that turned all those involved into comic book characters with superficial motives. Carolina squeezed my left hand and gave me a look that said to take the deal, so that we could be free of the whole thing.

"Everybody walks?" I asked.

"Everybody walks," he replied with a slight grin. Grayer knew the offer was too good for me not to give in.

Real-life courtrooms look a lot smaller than the ones on *Law and Order* and *The Practice.* The judges look more plain, less concerned with ideal justice than with getting through the day's case schedule. As the district attorney called me to the witness stand I didn't want to believe that I was there.

My whole misguided point had been to settle the matter in the streets, away from the blindfolded white lady with the scales in her hand who was always peeking through the cracks. I wanted to avoid the sketch artists and the media blitzes that tended to accompany any criminal charges against the hip-hop nation. I wanted to go home to my apartment without nosy reporters waiting on my front stoop. And to get that, all I had to do was point my finger at a man who was extremely guilty.

Still on crutches, I hobbled toward the witness box. The month leading up to the trial had been as blurry as a dream. All I was sure of was that no one had died and the bullet wound through TD's hand would heal. But it would leave a scar he'd brag about for the rest of his life. I took a seat up there, in the brightly lit room, wearing my still-new navy-blue suit, and prepared to do my part to bring the Dakota Grand/Mirage debacle to a close.

It turned out exactly the way I'd foreseen it back when I was in the hospital the first time. S-curl Ebony Man Randall Brown was the attorney. He sat quietly next to his client as the DA ran me through a series of questions that I swore to tell the whole truth about. Eventually I extended my right index finger towards the defendant.

Michael Adkins, a.k.a. Mirage, seemed much more human in the courtroom than he ever had onstage, in music videos, or standing directly in front of me with a mic in his hand at S.O.B.'s on that Friday night. His right arm was in a cast, his broken nose bandaged along with two broken fingers. Our war was something the industry talked about for much longer than the usual scandal. But it was still just a scandal.

He was facing twenty years for charges including attempted manslaughter, assault, and possession of an illegal firearm. But with a lawyer like Randall he'd probably be out in three, a year and a half with parole, maybe less. He never filed a civil suit against me. He didn't look me in the eye when I pointed him out. He barely recognized me when our eyes met briefly in a 7-Eleven five years afterwards.

I think it was because he was ashamed. Without Mirage, Michael Adkins was just another black man in a courtroom who'd committed a series of felonies. Without the name Dakota Grand I was just a guy who'd been a victim to his madness. The real verdict came from the judge, not us. And that was the way it should have been in the first place.

After the last answer to nitpicky questions that I no longer remember, I was told that I could leave the stand and return to my seat. But it took a moment for me to move. I didn't know why I had gone off the deep end that night, or during the days, weeks, and months before it. I couldn't understand why I hadn't seen the things that Scott and Carolina and everyone else had patiently tried to show me.

I wanted to dismiss it all as another terrible part of my former occupation. I wanted to say that it had come from listening to too many CDs, writing one paragraph too many about Delante Caution, who didn't take any shit from anyone. Maybe it was the consistently bad mix of weed and alcohol night after night on the same repeating scene. But upon the most thorough analysis, as I sat there, seated before the court, I knew that it had been about me holding on to an entire life that I had to let go of, and a name, that despite its intentions, was killing me slowly.

That moment was my point of total and complete clarity, after the hospital and the police inquiries, the press badgering and the numerous Hallmark cards from editors and opportunists alike. Despite everything I'd said and done, the words, the bullets and blows and explosions, it had all turned out the way everyone told me it would. I was the one left free and standing—hobbling actually—when the judge banged his gavel. The matter was finally closed and in the most basic way I had beaten him. But in truth, I had been my own greatest enemy.

The judge called for a recess and the court spiraled into disorder as I quickly made my way toward the exit. I didn't stop to speak to my attorney, or to Lamar, or to Maya, or even to Massai Morris on my way out. I just kept hobbling as fast as I could toward those two polished wood exit doors, where a mob of reporters was waiting. I maneuvered through them on my pair of wooden sticks, repeating "No comment" until I was clear of them. I couldn't wait to be rid of those damn crutches.

I was glad that there weren't a lot of TV cameras. I didn't want anyone to see me like that, especially my mother, who yelled at me through the phone for ten minutes because she'd had to find out about it all from the news. I hadn't wanted to tell anyone. I'd just wanted to get out of town before they ran me out on a rail.

"You ready?" Carolina asked me just beyond the police barricade in front of the courthouse. The outside of the building seemed deserted.

I'd told her that I didn't want her to be in the courtroom. I didn't want her to see the closing credits on Dakota Grand, Inc. But just then she was a sight for tired eyes. She had on these little hoop earrings and her hair was tied back in a ponytail. The smile she gave me was priceless.

"I'm very ready," I said as she hailed a car. A dingy yellow Lincoln was waiting for us and we got in. I kissed her deeply in the backseat as our Persian driver took us east, towards the midday sun, and more important JFK airport.

Before we even checked our bags, I knew that I wasn't coming back, at least not to the world where I had been before. I'd had the instincts once. But they'd gradually vanished like a picture from a frame, nothing left but the outline that held them in place. I closed my eyes in love's lap and waited to be delivered out of the wilderness.

SUMMER

GOT UP early to run and exercise down by the beach. On my way I nearly slipped on an old broom handle that was playing dead on the side of the road. I stopped and picked it up to examine it. The wood was olden and waterlogged as if the poor stick had spent most of its life being blown around in the rain. I carried it with me, determined to put it to use.

I didn't stop running for miles, until I came to the ocean, its clear waters sparkling in the light from the rising sun. It was a sight so beautiful that it had made me smile each time I saw it. I took off my shoes and walked down the beach to the shoreline. I took one end of the stick, placed it in the sand, and wrote in big letters: DAKOTA GRAND 1996–2000 R.I.P.

I drew a line under the short epitaph and walked into

the surf. The water was cool and invigorating. After a moment I stepped back onto the dry beach and walked past the words I'd written. A large wave crashed against the shore and washed them away like a forgotten memory.

Darrell Goodman. It was on my passport and my driver's license, my phone bill and the lease to my apartment. But it still felt strange. For too long *my* name had been lost like a package in the mail. Goodman wasn't fitting for the son of a convict who'd caught his third strike just before my sixteenth birthday. No one wanted to read anything written by a Goodman. And Darrell was too plain. The last thing I'd wanted was to be plain. I wanted to be grand. And I wanted to be away from everything that I knew, like those Dakota states out in the middle of nowhere.

I laughed. It was a running joke that had gotten away from me, from an entire industry and the music that supported it. I took a seat on the sand and watched the sun climb into the sky. The salty waves thrived on the streams of light coming down from above and I thought of Yemoja, the part of God that governs health and healing and children and the oceans of the world. Whenever I came to watch the waves I learned all over again why water was the most powerful element on earth. It both moved and halted, created and destroyed. I went in every morning to be a part of that power, the power that had brought me home.

"What took you so long?" Carolina asked from be-tween her mother's thick and flabby thighs. She was get-ting her hair braided so she wouldn't have to do it for the rest of the trip.

"I started watching the waves again," I said as I leaned down and gave her a kiss on the cheek. She looked up at my shoulder and down at the part of my leg my shorts didn't cover.

"The wounds are almost healed," she said.

"Looks like it," I replied.

"Well I'm glad that you're all in one piece again."

I think her parents wanted to like me but I was an American. And to them Americans were dangerous, for obvious reasons. But I always wondered if they would have acted differently had she brought home a white boy with the same job and the same problems. In the end it didn't make a difference because she loved me, and her parents knew that Carolina's love wasn't some-thing you picked up at any corner store around the way.

I had gotten used to Cuba in a month. We came in from Jamaica just a day after the trial came to a close. They didn't stamp our passports in Cuba so we were invisible to U.S. radar. Darrell Goodman liked that anonymity.

A movie studio had offered me $200,000 for the movie rights to *Caution*. And I took it. But I'd turned down twice as much to do a tell-all on the whole Mirage thing. Scott told me that some things were happening and that he might need another writer on a few projects. I told him I'd get back to him. But I wasn't sure about anything, at least when it came to work.

"Come here, Mr. Goodman," my baby said, enamored with her new name for me. She rose to her feet, her hair in perfect cornrows. Sistas at the shops back in Brooklyn would have been amazed by what Cubans could do.

I walked over and took her hand. She clasped mine tightly and we walked up the long country road toward Santiago to visit her older cousins who lived somewhere in that direction. Later in the day I went down to the beach with her little brother Ibrahim and watched him build a castle in the sand just beyond the tide line. The image was much different in reality than it had been in Dakota Grand's electric subway dreams.

I enjoyed sitting there and watching him, an eight-year-old more curious than George. He was young and creative and focused and smart. And when he was building his castles he was happy. After everything so was I. That had made it all worth it.

ABOUT THE AUTHOR

Kenji Jasper is a writer and journalist whose work has appeared in *Vibe, Essence, The Source,* and other publications. His first novel, *Dark,* was published by Broadway Books in 2001. A native of Washington, D.C., and a graduate of Morehouse College, he now lives in Brooklyn.